TARGET: EARTH

BY JOHNNY MARCIANO
AND EMILY CHENOWETH

KLAWDE

EVIL ALIEN WARLORD CAT

ILLUSTRATED BY
ROBB
MOMMAERTS

PENGUIN WORKSHOP

My name is Raj. I'm a regular kid from Brooklyn who just moved across the country to Elba, Oregon. I hated it when I was forced to come here, but now I kind of like it. I have a mom, a dad, and a very special cat–Klawde!

RAJ

KLAWDE

My name is not Klawde. It is Lord High Emperor Wyss-Kuzz, the Magnificent. I was exiled across the universe to this backward planet of furless ogres known as Earth. I hated it when I was forced to come here, and now I hate it even more.

CHAPTER 0

Perched upon the dining table, I gazed out over a scene of destruction. I had shredded a pillow, mutilated a houseplant, and toppled every vase I could find.

Usually such random acts of violence did much to improve my mood. Today, however, they did nothing to curb my rage.

Though I had suffered endless humiliations from the moment I set paw on this miserable planet, nothing—not living with ogres, having to lick my own fur, or being repeatedly betrayed by my enemies—could compare to the news I had received three moonrises ago. On my home planet, I was being called Wyss-Kuzz the . . . the . . . *Dog Lover.*

Hiss!

I was about to do something truly terrible when the communicator rang. I raced down to the bunker. My minion, Flooffee-Fyr, was calling.

"Tell me quickly," I said. "Have you yet convinced the felines of Lyttyrboks that I am not friends with that despicable spacemutt?"

"Um . . . well, not really, Supreme Leader."

"Does this mean that they are still calling me Wyss-Kuzz the—*hack hack*—Dog Lover?"

"Oh no," Flooffee said, brightening. "They're not

calling you that at all anymore."

My rage softened. My hopes soared. Finally, the mood of the mob had turned!

"They're more calling you, uh . . ." Flooffee paused. "Well . . . now they're calling you Wyss-Kuzz the Butt-Sniffer."

It took all my training—all the discipline in my warrior soul—not to begin a new rampage of destruction. My claws pulsed with the urge to wreak havoc. I had not felt **fury** like this in—*in*—well, in at least five minutes.

Flooffee blinked stupidly at me.

"What?" I roared. "Why are you looking at me like that?"

"Um, I was just wondering?" he said. "Is it true?"

"Is *what* true?"

"Have you ever sniffed a dog's butt?"

HISSSS!

"Or Flabby's butt?"

I hung up on the infuriating fool and went upstairs to take a Focus Nap.

Upon reaching this state of higher feline consciousness, certain facts became clear to me. My current reputation made the reconquest of Lyttyrboks impossible at present. But in the meantime, it was crucial that I keep my conquesting skills sharp. If I didn't, what would Generalissima Zok say at the next meeting of the Allied Warlords of Evil club? It was imperative that I vanquish a planet—*any* planet, no matter how vile or backward it might be.

This, naturally, led me to think of Earth.

CHAPTER 1

"Klawde!" I yelled as I came inside and dropped my backpack in the hall. "Where are you?"

There was no answer, so I grabbed a handful of potato chips and went upstairs. He was asleep on my pillow, and considering the mood he'd been in lately, I decided not to wake him. Besides, I could hardly wait to open my computer and get online. Because *today* was the day the new VisionQuest Ultra was being released!

The VQ Ultra was the best virtual reality headset money could buy. It was insanely light, wireless, and it came with six motion sensors that tracked your every move. It even had a connected drone, which you could control with the headset. *I had to buy the VQ Ultra!* The only problem was how much it cost.

It was **$1,286**—and that was just for the headset.

With all the cool accessories, it cost twice as much.

How would I ever come up with that kind of money? My allowance was ten bucks a week, and that was only if I actually did all my chores.

I tortured myself watching launch videos of the VQ Ultra until my computer crashed. I rebooted it, and five minutes later the stupid thing crashed again. It was Mom's old laptop—from, like, before I was born—and it barely worked for anything but email.

Luckily, I had a cat who could help fix it.

"Hey, Klawde—"

"No."

"Come on, Klawde. Please?"

He growled at me. "I am exceedingly busy."

"Busy? You've been sleeping this whole time!"

"Incorrect. I was engaged in a Focus Nap, followed by a Strategy Nap—two of the nine fundamental nap states."

"Please?" I begged him. "My computer keeps crashing."

Klawde flicked his tail. "Ask in the proper manner."

I sighed. I hated when he made me do this.

"O All-Powerful Lord and Master, can you please assist a lowly, furless, pathetic Human and fix this computer?"

"That was better," he said. "Let me consider it. *No*."

CHAPTER 2

Earth was hardly worth conquering, of course, as it was small, teeming with ogres, and in a particularly unattractive corner of the universe. This was why none of the other members of the Allied Warlords of Evil had bothered to vanquish it.

Still, I needed *something* to occupy my time between naps.

As I pondered how to crush Earth, however, certain problems presented themselves. Most signficantly, no matter how feeble the Human mind might be, the Human body was immensely strong.

Since these ogres could not be subjugated by brute force, I would need to use my superior feline brain. As the ancients say, *'Tis not the sharp claw, but the sharp mind that makes the victor.*

I was considering my options when the boy-Human interrupted me with his latest complaint about his internet-access device. He wanted me to repair it, but its technology was almost incomprehensibly crude. He might as well hand me two sticks and expect me to create nuclear fusion.

"For what pointless Human purpose do you need this machine?"

He explained that he wanted to watch videos of something called the VisionQuest Ultra. Placed upon one's head, he informed me, this instrument allowed its wearer to see, hear, and act in any environment that could be imagined.

"They call it virtual reality," he said. "And I want it."

"Well of course *you* would want to escape your reality," I said.

He failed to understand my biting wit.

"It's like you're in a different world, in someone

else's body," he said. "And you're controlling everything they do."

My whiskers twitched.

"*Controlling* them, you say?"

The boy then brought out his phone so that we could watch a video advertising the device. As the capacity of this wearable technology became clear, my fur began to stand on end. Could this cumbersome Human gadget be repurposed for my own ends?

It was extremely primitive, of course. And yet it was not unlike the devices we used to manage our worker robots back on Lyttyrboks. And then it struck me. The Zom-Beam! My most brilliant creation! If I paired this Human apparatus with the Zom-Beam's mind-controlling psylo-waves, this pathetic planet would be mine for the taking!

"Ogre, let us get this device," I said. "RIGHT NOW."

CHAPTER 3

I had to explain to Klawde that getting the VQ Ultra wasn't that simple.

"What do you mean?" he said. "Just go to the virtual reality store and seize it!"

"First of all, there is no 'virtual reality store,'" I said. "And second of all, even if there was, we couldn't just take it."

Klawde's tail swished. "But that is how one gets things," he said. "By taking them from others."

"Maybe on Lyttyrboks," I said. "But here on Earth, if you want something, you have to pay for it."

"Ogre, it is only my enemies who must pay."

"I'm not talking about revenge, Klawde," I said. "I'm talking about money."

"Money!" Klawde spat. "What is this 'money' you

ogres endlessly babble on about, anyway?"

I didn't really know how to explain money to a cat, even one who was smarter than me.

"It's sort of like trading," I said. "Sometimes I trade old comics with friends. But if I want a new comic, I have to go to a store and give them money. So basically I trade money for the comic."

"Ah, so this 'money' is of high value," Klawde said. "Is it delicious food? Exotic feathers? A pawheld particle accelerator?"

"Uh, no," I said, pulling a crumpled dollar bill out of my pocket. "It's this."

CHAPTER 4

The concept of trading I understood, as it is practiced in all the inhabited galaxies. But everywhere else, one trades items of equal value—say, a Torgrassian torpedo for an exuviating robot. Or, as in the case of the squirrel mercenaries of the planet Wuud, nuts for their military service.

But "money"—what *was* it?

The boy-ogre reached into one of the storage pouches located in his leg-coverings and pulled out a small piece of paper. "This is a dollar."

I had seen these green rectangles covered with crude Human scribblings before. Naturally, I had assumed they were portraits of particularly ugly relatives of theirs. But they were for trade? For payment?

"But it's just paper," I said. "It is worthless."

"Well, it's not worthless to humans, because we all want it." He held up more of these green rectangles with ancient ogres on them. "If you took all these to the grocery store, you could buy a pound of butter and a carton of milk. If you had twelve hundred eighty-six of them, you could buy a VQ Ultra."

"So let me see if I have this correct. These 'dollars' are abstract credits that Humans trade with one another because you simply *agree* that they are worth something?"

"Pretty much, yeah."

A system based on trust? No wonder we did not use dollars on Lyttyrboks.

"Is money the only thing we can use to purchase the technology?"

"It's the only way to get pretty much anything."

Although the very notion of these dollars disgusted me, this "VQ" could well be the missing piece to my

Zom-Beam, the prototype of which remained buried in my litter box command center. If I could link the headset controller, the flying drone, and the Zom-Beam's mind-controlling rays, I could strike any target I chose from the comfort of my own bunker!

"Fine, ogre," I said. "Tell me how we acquire the dollars we need."

"Well, the very best way of getting money," the boy-ogre said, "is to get your parents to give you some."

CHAPTER 5

"Absolutely **not**," Mom said. "You just had a birthday."

"I'll pay you back," I said. "I swear."

"You'll pay me back over *twelve hundred dollars*?" Mom crossed her arms. "How?"

I didn't have an answer to that question.

"Sit down, Raj," she said. "I think we should have a little talk."

Ugh. I *hated* Mom's talks.

"Money, Raj," Mom said, "is something that we *earn*." After that, my ears pretty much shut off. She was saying something about how a penny saved is a penny earned—which makes no sense—when Dad walked into the kitchen.

"You need a little extra money, son? You could do

some extra chores," he said. "Like make me a peanut-butter-and-banana sandwich!"

Mom and I both rolled our eyes.

"With the way you guys pay me for chores, I'll be ancient by the time I make enough to buy the VQ," I said. "Like *your* age."

"Well, I know one way you can make money, and it's not even a chore," Mom said. "Have a yard sale. We've only lived in this house a few months, and somehow it's already completely filled with junk." She glared at Dad.

"We haven't even unpacked everything yet!" he said.

"If you haven't needed it by now, Krish," Mom said, "then you don't need it at all."

"But somewhere in one of those boxes is my handheld, battery-operated milk frother! I bought it when I was in dental school, and I still haven't had the chance to use it."

"Which only proves my point," Mom said.

"But I need it for when I open my Italian-style cafe," he said. "Krish's Koffee!"

Mom turned to me. "Raj, if it's in a moving box, you can sell it."

CHAPTER 6

On what the Humans call "Saturday," the boy-ogre began to lay out items on a large table in the driveway. I was pleased to see how much he was finding to sell. However worthless these articles would seem to any sensible being in the universe, surely other ogres would pay many dollars for them. And then we would possess vast riches!

"Let us also get rid of that hideous rope sculpture," I said, as I watched him attach tiny pieces of sticky paper—"price tags," he called them—to the objects.

"You mean the scratching post Dad bought you?"

"It is useless to me," I said. "I prefer his shins."

The boy-ogre next went to a corner of the garage where dozens of cardboard boxes were stacked.

"Ah, a fine idea for making dollars!" I said. "These

sleeping chambers must be worth a fortune." As far as I was concerned, they were the only thing of value in this barbarian wasteland.

"Not so much," he said. "It's the stuff inside them that might be worth something."

The boy-ogre gazed into one, and an especially pitiful look came over his face.

"Brownie," he said.

The boy-ogre held up what appeared to be a small species of bear, the likes of which I had never seen before. I sank into Defensive Crouch. Had the beast been hibernating? Was it still alive?

It was not. But perhaps it once had been, and the Humans had preserved its body.

"It's my old teddy bear," the boy-ogre said. He reached into the box again. "And here's the monkey I got for my sixth birthday, and the penguin I won at the fair . . ."

Here was yet another bizarre Human quirk. Certainly no feline kept boxes of stuffed ogres around. Then again, I could understand why Humans would want to possess models of their superiors.

"These animals—do they have a high value?"

"They do," the boy-ogre said. "*Sentimental* value."

"This 'sentimental' value—it means we will acquire additional dollars?"

"No," the boy-ogre said, staring into the plastic eyes of his bear. "It means it is worth more to me than to anyone else. Isn't that right, Brownie?"

I slashed the bear out of his hands. "Sell it!"

The sooner I accumulated this Human money, the sooner I could purchase the technology I needed to repurpose my Zom-Beam into a weapon of awesome power—and commence my conquest of this sorry excuse for a planet.

CHAPTER 7

All the other stuffed animals were tagged and set out, but I just couldn't bring myself to put a price on Brownie. What kind of person sells their teddy bear?

"What's that you got there, Raj?"

It was Lindy, walking over from across the street.

"Aww, look at this guy!" she said, pulling the bear out of my hands. "He's a little dirty and—*sniff sniff*—kinda smelly, but he'd scrub up nice. He looks like a Cuddles! Do you like that name, little bear?"

"*His name is Brownie,*" I said under my breath.

The front door banged open, and Dad came out of the house carrying a mug of coffee and a folding chair.

"You coming to help, Dad?" I called.

He laughed. "Ho no! Just watching, son. You're doing a great job." He took a slurp of his coffee as he settled into his seat. "It's a wonderful day for a yard sale, isn't it!"

"Hey Raj, what's this?" Lindy asked.

My dad looked up, saw what she was pointing at, and immediately shot out of his chair.

"Whoa whoa whoa, Raj—what do you think you're doing putting *that* out for sale?"

"The broken lava lamp?"

"Yes, the lava lamp! You can't sell that." He snatched it off the table and cradled it in his arms like a baby. "Sorry, Lindy," he said. "I had this in my college dorm room, and it's like it's a part of me."

Then Dad started pulling other things off the table.

"My magnetic paper clips! And my *molar bear* mug!"

"Dad," I said, "can you just go back to your chair, please?"

In the end, Lindy decided to buy my old Monopoly game. I told her it was missing half of the money, but she didn't care. She handed me two dollars.

"I'm your first sale!"

I took her money and opened my laptop. Mom wanted me to enter every purchase into a spreadsheet—"It will be a good lesson if you ever start your own business!"—but my stupid computer was acting up again.

"My mom can totally fix that. She, like, does computer stuff for a living," Lindy said. "I can take it to my house right now!"

"Sure," I said. "Thanks."

After Lindy, we had no customers for a while, and I was starting to worry that the yard sale would be a disaster. But suddenly a whole bunch of people showed up, and all of them bought something. Well, all of them except Mr. Wallace from down the street.

"FIVE dollars for *this*? You want FIVE dollars?" he asked, holding up an unopened box of headphones. "Why not just go rob a bank?"

Grumpy neighbors aside, I was feeling pretty good about how things were going—until I heard the scrape of skateboards on the sidewalk. I knew who it was before I even looked up.

"I thought this was supposed to be a yard sale, not a *junk* sale," Scorpion said. "What's the matter? The garbage company wouldn't take any of this *garbage*?"

Scorpion laughed way too loudly at his dumb joke and tried to high-five Newt, who clearly didn't find it funny.

"We sold all the good stuff already," I mumbled.

"Awwww, look at this!" Scorpion said, pointing to

my animals. "Are these the baby's *stuffies*?"

"This one's kind of cute," Newt said, picking up

Brownie. I was surprised. But then again, every once in a

while Newt did say something nice.

"What*ever*," Scorpion said.

"How much do you want for him?" Newt said.

She seemed to really like the teddy bear. And what was I hanging on to Brownie for, anyway? He lived in a box in our garage.

"Aw, just take him," I said.

"Thanks," she said.

Newt stepped off the curb and laid Brownie facedown in the middle of the street. Then she ran over him with her skateboard.

Scorpion laughed. "Sweet!" he said. "Let ME try!"

Klawde leaned in to my ear. "I have skinned enemies alive for lesser transgressions."

For once, I didn't think he was being unreasonable.

CHAPTER 8

The "yard sale" was long and tedious, but by the end of the day, my Human and I had a large stack of green paper rectangles, plus many silver coins.

The boy-Human shuffled through the dollars, counting them.

"We must be extremely wealthy!" I exclaimed, purring.

"We made fifty-seven dollars," he said. "Probably sixty with the quarters and dimes."

"Excellent! What can that buy us?" Surely at least *one* weapons-building drone.

"Maybe dinner," the boy-ogre said, shrugging. "At Bob's Pizza Palace."

I spat in contempt. "What a waste of naptimes! We must sell things of greater value. What of the motorized vehicles? Can we sell the fortress? Certainly that would be worth many *hundreds* of dollars."

"We can't sell our house, Klawde. We live in it."

This was infuriating. "If we can't sell our way to riches, how else can we make money?"

"Well," the boy-ogre said, "there's work."

"What do you mean by 'work'?" I asked. "Is that anything like napping? Scratching? Destroying the fortress of your enemy? Because that would be a most fun way to make dollars."

"Work is the exact opposite of fun," he said. "It's when you spend a long time doing something you don't want to do—something that's really hard or really boring. Usually both."

This work was the most horrible Human concept yet.

"No cat would ever do anything they didn't want to do," I said. "Unless their warlord forced them to."

"Well, here on Earth, no one can force you to do

things for them," he said. "They have to give you money. Like how Lindy gets paid to walk Mr. Mitchell's dog."

That was an odious task indeed. One could smell the brute from a block away. "So you are saying that all wealthy people became rich by working?"

"Well, no," the boy-ogre said. "*Really* rich people are usually born that way. And other people get rich when their grandparents or whoever die and leave them a fortune."

This sounded promising.

"Perhaps *you* have a wealthy loved one or ancient relative near death?" I asked.

Alas, he did not.

CHAPTER 9

I'd finally cleaned up the last of the leftover yard-sale junk when Cedar and Steve rode up on their bikes.

"How'd it go, Raj?" Cedar asked.

"Yeah," Steve said. "How much money did you make?"

"Sixty-one dollars," I said. "And thirty-five cents."

"Wow," he said. "That's *it*?"

"Yeah," I said. "And I have to give half of it to my parents."

"But you did all the work yourself," Cedar said. "They aren't even here!"

"My dad was, uh, supervising."

Just then Dad came walking out of the house carrying a glass of iced tea and wearing an enormous pair of headphones. He settled back into his chair and waved at us.

"Hey, Dr. Krish," Cedar and Steve both said.

"HI, KIDS," Dad shouted. "MAN, THANK GOODNESS THAT'S OVER! IT'S HARD WORK RUNNING A YARD SALE!"

He leaned back and crossed his legs.

"At this rate I'll have to have forty more garage sales to buy that headset," I said.

"Maybe you could get a job," Steve suggested.

"Don't you have to be in high school to do that?" I asked.

"Hey, I have an idea!" Cedar said. "How about we start a business? It's fall cleanup time, so we can rake leaves and clear gutters and stuff. There's a kid on my block who paid for his car that way. We can split the work *and* the money!"

"Then you can get that virtual reality headset you're always talking about," Steve said.

"And I can get the telescope I want," Cedar said. "The Astro 9000!"

"Well I know I need *my* lawn raked!"

I turned and saw Lindy's mom walking across the street with my laptop. She explained that she had defragged the system, removed some grayware—whatever that meant—and doubled the memory. "It should work a lot better now," she said, handing it to me.

"Wow, thanks, Mrs. Langston!"

She gave me a big smile. "Please, call me Annie." Then she held out a Ziploc bag. "Anyone want cookies?"

"They're still warm," Steve whispered.

I was taking a second cookie when Annie cleared her throat. "Um, Raj, I have to say that your search history is rather . . . *interesting.*" She looked at me sort of sideways. "I'm sorry to have looked, but I wanted to see if you'd visited any suspicious sites. Your computer was so slow that I was worried you'd downloaded some malware by mistake."

I stopped chewing. "For real?"

"I didn't find any viruses, thankfully," she said. "But why were you googling things like 'how to conquer earth' and 'weaponized squirrels'?"

"I didn't search for any of that," I said.

"Really?" She looked skeptical. "Then why would it be on your computer?"

"I have no idea!" I said.

Except wait—I did.

Klawde.

That cat was going to get me into serious trouble someday.

"Oh. Huh," she said. "Well, in the future, you do need to be careful about the sites you visit. You don't want a cryptoworm."

That *did* sound scary. "Okay. Thanks again for fixing it," I said.

As she crossed the street to go home, she turned back. "And I'm serious about the lawn," she said. "With Oliver away on his foreign exchange program and my husband always traveling for work, it's more than Lindy and I can handle. I'll pay twenty dollars an hour for the three of you."

Cedar, Steve, and I all high-fived each other.

"That's so awesome!" Steve said. "That's like ten dollars an hour for each of us!"

"It's actually not," I said.

"We have to make flyers! And a logo!" Cedar said.

"It'll be so fun!"

"Yeah! Well, except for the yard work part," I said. "But I'll do it for the VQ."

Cedar turned to Steve. "You never said what *you* want to buy."

"I don't know," he said, shrugging. "But if I spent it all on *Frogger* at Quarterworld, I bet I'd finally get the high score!"

Cedar patted his arm. "You just keep thinking about it," she said.

CHAPTER 10

My nineteenth nap of the day resulted in a brilliant idea. (The ancients were right: A feline's best thinking *does* only happen after the first eighteen.)

It was simple, really. I would just manufacture the money myself. Primitive though the ogre's scanner and printer were, they could transfer images from one flat sheet of crushed-up trees to another. And since these dollars were nothing more than green rectangles of this paper, I could print as many of them as I wanted! I would use them to buy the VQ Ultra, as well as all the rest of the technology I needed.

Purr.

But when I explained my plan to the boy-ogre, he shook his head.

"It doesn't work like that, Klawde," he said. "Only

governments can print money. If you copy it, it's called counterfeiting. And that is totally against the law."

Such absurd Human regulations obviously did not apply to me—I was hardly a citizen of this pathetic planet—but the boy-ogre explained that no store would accept homemade dollars.

Hiss! Of course the petty warlords of Earth kept such a mighty tool to themselves. How frustrating that you must actually *have* power before you can abuse it.

"So how do I become a government so that I may print money?"

"Forget it, Klawde," the boy-ogre said.

I did not understand why he was always so negative.

"By the way," he added, "do you know that you almost totally blew your cover? When Lindy's mom was fixing my laptop, she saw my search history—*your* search history."

He opened his computer and turned the screen toward me.

> weapons-building drones

> brainwashing technologies

> are humans edible?

> long-term effects of earth's toxic atmosphere on the cerebellum

"Why were you looking up this stuff, anyway?" he demanded.

I swished my tail. "Because *you* don't have any of the answers."

The ogre just shook his head and sighed.

I hated when he did that.

CHAPTER 11

Sunday was the first day of the Three Gardeneers Lawn Care Company.

The name was most definitely not my idea. Or Cedar's. But *The Three Musketeers* was Steve's favorite old movie, and he won rock-paper-scissors on what to call us.

"*The Three Musketeers* is about these three really cool friends with swords who, like, do good deeds and stuff," Steve explained. "And we're friends, and there are three of us!"

He held his rake like it was a sword and slashed it through the air.

"It's a terrible name, but whatever," Cedar said as we fanned out across Lindy's yard.

We'd barely even gotten started when Steve stopped

to take his first water break. Cedar, meanwhile, raced an old-fashioned mower—the kind that doesn't have a motor—back and forth across the yard. And I was doing my best with the raking, even though I kept sneezing and having to stop to blow my nose.

"I think Raj is allergic to yard work," Steve called down from the tree he was sitting in.

"Actually, it looks like *you* are," Cedar said. "How about you get off your butt and start pulling up that crabgrass?"

By the time we were done with all the mowing, raking, and weeding, it was way past lunchtime. Cedar had blisters, my nose was so stuffed up I could barely breathe, and Steve . . . well, Steve was Steve. He kept trying to get us to play Three Musketeers with rake handles, and when we wouldn't, he lay down in the grass next to Flabby Tabby. They both had their eyes closed now and were sunning their bellies.

"Aw, it's like Steve is a cat, too!" Lindy said, walking out of the house with a tray of lemonade.

Lindy could be annoying, but right now I was really glad to see her. The lemonade was delicious.

She smiled at us. "I was the first customer at your yard sale, and now I'm the first customer of your yard business. Or my mom is, anyway. Pretty cool, huh?"

"Totally," I said, pressing the cold glass to my hot cheek. It felt great.

CHAPTER 12

The boy-ogre came in looking tired and extremely dirty.

"Are you *raking* in the money, ogre?"

"Ha ha ha, very funny," he said, wiping his nose on the back of his sleeve.

"What is that leaking out of your nostrils?" I asked. "Are those your brains? Are you going to die? If you do, will I inherit your money?"

"I have allergies."

I did not know what these were, but I assumed they were not worth dollars. "How much money did you earn today, ogre?"

"Twenty dollars. But I didn't even get it. When we were done, Lindy's mom realized she didn't have any cash in the house. She asked if we took credit cards, which we obviously don't. Then she offered to pay us in cybermoney." He sniffled. "I think she was joking."

When I asked him what "cybermoney" was, the boy-ogre shrugged. "I think it's actually called 'cryptcurrency' or something."

A search on the ogre's "web browser" revealed to me that cryptocurrency was virtual money, and that it was made up of digital code instead of green paper. And it was not controlled by governments—individual Humans could create these currencies. They simply needed unbreakable encryption and vast computing power.

Of course, the computing power here on Earth was pitiful compared to that of Lyttyrboks, and the Humans' encrypted files were kitten's play to unlock. And so (with minor assistance from Flooffee) I could create a vastly more secure and thus more valuable cryptocurrency than any ogre could.

In other words, I **could** make my own money!

I immediately descended to the bunker to call my minion.

"Oh, hey there, Supremest Butt-Sniffer!" Flooffee-Fyr answered. "Er, I mean, All Powerfullest Warlord."

My plan had lifted my spirits so high that I let the insult pass.

It took me some time to explain Human paper money, but Flooffee grasped cryptocurrency instantly. "Oh, it's just encrypted code?"

"Barely," I said. "It only runs to one hundred thousand lines."

"Is that all?" Flooffee said.

"I know," I said. "Pathetic."

"If you want something really unbreakable, I have that eight-to-the-billionth-power encryption we used to send orders to Colonel Akorn's mercenaries during the War of Wall-Nutz. It uses a super-nifty Torg algorithm, and it's got a Gallassian block cipher with—"

"Don't talk to me about it," I said. "Start coding!"

"Okay, O Grandest Leader," he said. "No problemo. What are you going to name your money, anyway?"

I purred. "I shall call it . . . **KitKoin**!"

After all, "K" *is* the Humans' most interesting letter.

CHAPTER 13

In the week and a half that the Three Gardeneers Lawn Care Company had been in business, I felt like I never stopped moving. Because in addition to the stuff I always had to do—homework, clubs, and chores—I also worked with Cedar and Steve every day. We bagged leaves, cleared brush, spread mulch, cleaned gutters, and pulled weeds till our fingers cramped. It was miserable. *I* was miserable. My nose ran constantly and I always felt tired and hungry.

So when I got home from raking up Mr. Wallace's yard after school on Thursday, I collapsed onto the couch.

Mom was rushing around, getting ready for some kind of smart-person awards dinner.

"I must praise your industriousness, Raj," she said

as she kissed me goodbye. "Such initiative will one day be rewarded!"

That's what I'd been hoping for, but the reward wasn't coming fast enough. Even though it seemed like we were making a ton of money, split three ways it was not a lot. And my mom had decided that since I had a "new revenue stream," I should buy my own ice cream and comics. Who knew that a rainbow sprinkle waffle cone with two scoops could cost six bucks?

I'd counted my money this morning and all I had was $117. At this rate, I'd have to work for a year before I could buy the VQ Ultra.

Dad wandered into the living room wearing a hat I was sure I had sold at the garage sale. "I'm mighty proud of you, too, son," he said. "I can tell you're working really hard."

"Yeah," I said. "But I'm still not making that much."

Dad's face lit up. "Well, I can help you out with that."

"Like with a loan?" I asked hopefully.

"With more work!" he said. "I've got some great ideas for those extra chores I was telling you about, buddy." He sat down and wrote out a list.

"You want me to sort your baseball card collection? And make you a snack when you get home from work?" I said. "And help you put on your *socks*?"

"My back is so stiff in the mornings that it's hard to bend over," he said defensively. "And, you know, you should make yourself a snack, too."

I shook my head no—until he handed me a ten. "Here's an advance."

"Fine," I said.

"Just don't tell your mother," he said.

"That'll cost you extra."

Dad laughed, but I was serious.

"Now, how about you get off that couch and make us some popcorn?"

CHAPTER 14

It had been a trying ten moonrises.

My minion, working at his typical plodding pace, had taken three of them to create the most sophisticated virtual money Earth had ever seen. Yet somehow the Humans did not race to purchase my currency.

It was not until I bombarded online news outlets with the propaganda the Humans call a "press release" that the ogres began to take notice.

Now sales were moving briskly. Checking my account, I was pleased to note that I had made well over $100,000.

In the last hour.

My good mood was somewhat dampened by the wheezing sound of the boy-ogre trudging up the stairs. He was muddy and exhausted, with his brains again leaking out of his nose.

"You really should get that looked at," I said.

He fell facedown upon the sleeping platform and told me how much money he had made today.

"Wow, fifteen *entire* dollars," I said. "How very impressive."

In the six seconds it had taken me to speak, I calculated that I had made $168.

The boy-ogre might not be getting the VQ Ultra anytime soon. But I could think of someone who would be.

Purr.

CHAPTER 15

On Sunday morning, a phone call woke me up. I covered my head with my pillow, but whoever it was kept calling. Didn't they know it was the weekend?

"*Steve*," I said, finally picking up. "Why are you calling me so early?"

"Early?" he said. "It's after ten! We were supposed to be at the new job already. Didn't you get all my texts?"

I groaned.

"I'm on your porch, by the way."

Grumbling, I went downstairs and let Steve in. While he read an old copy of Americaman, I got dressed, shoved a pack of Kleenex into my pocket, and took some allergy medicine. We met Cedar in front of her house, and then the three of us biked to a neighborhood I hadn't been to before. Cedar told me it was called

Waterloo, and it was where all the rich kids lived.

"Here's the place!" Steve said, stopping in front of a huge leaf-covered lawn.

"Whoa," Cedar said, grinning. "We're going to make a serious payday."

But then she looked at the name on the mailbox, and her expression changed.

"Hold on," she said, "please tell me this is not—"

"What's up, losers!"

"—*Scorpion's* yard!"

A narrow, mean face was peering down at us from an attic window.

"Have fun cleaning up after T-Rex, nerds!" he yelled.

I looked closer at the yard. The grass was high, but it didn't hide the giant piles of poop.

Steve turned to me in horror. "Does Scorpion have an actual dinosaur?"

A man walked out of the house who must have

been Scorpion's dad, even though he looked totally nice and normal. "Hey, kids," he said. "Glad you could make it. My son said I should call you because you could really use the money. Pretty thoughtful of him, huh?"

Yeah, real thoughtful.

"Before we rake, sir, there's a lot of . . . um, extra stuff in the yard," I said.

"What do you mean?" he asked.

"It's, well . . ." Cedar said.

"Your yard is full of mountains of **dog poop**!" Steve blurted out.

Scorpion's dad squinted into the grass, then turned to the window that Scorpion's head was still poking out of. "Son, when was the last time you scooped the poop?" he hollered up.

Scorpion shrugged. "I don't know, a few months ago. Who cares? These *Gardeneers* can take care of it."

"Son, poop-scooping is *your* job, and T-Rex is *your*

Great Dane," his father said firmly. "Come down here this instant. I hired your friends to pick up leaves, not doggie doo-doo."

Scorpion let out a scream of disgust as his face disappeared from the window and he slammed it shut.

"Gee, thanks, Mr. Scorpion," Steve said.

"Mr. *Who*?" he asked.

"Nothing!" Cedar said quickly. "We appreciate your business, sir."

CHAPTER 16

1 KitKoin = 898.31 dollars . . . 1 KitKoin = 901.17 dollars . . . 1 KitKoin = 902.99 dollars . . . 1 KitKoin = 904.08 dollars . . .

The numbers crawled across the bottom of the screen as the LootCounter app monitored the meteoric rise of my currency. It was a most pleasing thing to watch.

My communicator rang. Normally I loathed interruptions—particularly when coming from Flooffee-Fyr—but this time I did not mind, as it is hard to brag only to oneself.

"Greetings, flunky," I said. "No doubt you are calling to praise me for my brilliance."

"Uh . . . not so much, actually," he said. "I mean, I'm sure we can get to that and all. But first I was wondering—"

"Thanks to KitKoin, every few naptimes I make tens of *thousands* of dollars."

"Is that a lot?"

"I'm not sure. But I think I am extremely rich."

"That's, uh, really great," he said. "But I called with a question? I'm—"

"You are wanting me to reveal the true reason I desire so many Earth dollars!"

"Actually, Your Masterfulness, I—"

"Well, I will tell you. I have discovered ogre technology that will allow me to execute my *newest* evil scheme, which is actually an old evil scheme. Do you remember . . . the ZOM-BEAM?"

"Of course I do," Flooffee said. "I'm the one who created it, O Overreaching Master."

"*You* created it? Hah!" I scoffed. "You may have designed it, but it was *I* who managed to fashion one here on Earth out of the junk of the ogres."

"*Well, it's not like it worked . . . ,*" he muttered under his breath.

I ignored his insolence. "My new Zom-Beam will function perfectly once it is finished. Many expensive, high-precision instruments have already been delivered by the brown-suited ogre who drives the box truck. However, the most important component—the VQ Ultra—is stuck on planet Back Order."

The good news was that the technology was finally

supposed to arrive tomorrow. I only hoped that the delivery ogre would again come while the Humans were gone.

I allowed myself a small purr of satisfaction. "I had forgotten how much fun it is to make plans to conquer a planet—even one as backward as this."

"Okay, well, getting back to why I called, I just have one *quick* question before—"

"I must say I find myself almost feeling affection for Earth," I went on. "These are its last days of independence, Flooffee. Soon the entire world will be *mi*—"

"ALL-POWERFUL LEADER! Which one of Lyttyrboks's eighty-seven moons is your favorite?"

"What?"

"I said, which one of the eighty-seven moons—"

"I heard you," I said. "And the question is absurd because the answer is so patently obvious. My favorite is number sixty-three."

After all, did any *other* moon have over thirty thousand species of plump, flightless birds?

"Now where was I?" I said. "Oh, yes. Soon the entire world will be *mine*!"

CHAPTER 17

As I passed Lindy's house on the way home from school on Monday, her mom waved me over and handed me three crisp twenty-dollar bills, one for each of the Gardeneers. "I'm so sorry I made you wait to get paid, Raj. Like I said, I never seem to have actual *cash* in my wallet."

My parents said that all the time, but it was usually because they didn't want to buy me stuff.

"It's a good thing you don't charge in KitKoin," she said. "Otherwise what I owe you from last week would be a whole lot more today!"

"KitKoin?" I said.

"Oh, sorry—computer nerd alert!" She made a goofy face and an alarm sound. "Blockchain technology, crypto markets, hash-based signature trees—they fascinate me."

I didn't understand a single word of what she'd just said. She kept on talking, though, and I did pick up that KitKoin was a new kind of cybercurrency that had gotten super popular, super fast.

"And no one even knows who created it," she said. "It's all very mysterious."

"It sounds cool," I said.

"Cool, yes. But also a bit troubling," she said. "When you have a new global currency and its founder is anonymous, you have to hope they are not a *hostile entity*." Then she smiled brightly. "But look at me, going on and on about this stuff! I tell you what, if you want to make a little more of that good old-fashioned paper money, you and your crew can clean my gutters."

"Oh, sure," I said. "We'll get on that right away."

When I turned to go home, I saw a UPS truck parked in front of my house. I caught the delivery guy as he was leaving a stack of packages on our porch. "You need me to sign?" I asked.

He looked at the order. "Nope. No signature required. Raj Banerjee does live here, right?"

"Uh, yeah."

The guy smiled. "That's good, because I've been leaving boxes for him all week."

That was weird. Packages for *me*?

I looked down, and sure enough, every single one of them had my name on it. I opened the one on top and—

No freaking way.

I ran inside the house, leaving a trail of styrofoam peanuts on the floor behind me. But I didn't believe it was real until I was holding it in my hands.

The VQ Ultra!

I yelped—I actually yelped. And jumped up in the air.

It was the entire VQ UltraMax suite! With all six motion sensors. And the noise-canceling earphones! And—*whoa!*—the last box was the ultra-lightweight

auto-sync seeing-eye drone!

I called my dad right away.

"Dad!" I said when he picked up. "You're the best! Did you get all this for me because I took off your socks? Or because of all the snacks? Thank you **so much**!"

"I got you *what* now?"

I told him, and he said he had nothing to do with it.

"Your mother would be furious with me if I got you all that. Besides," he started to whisper, *"I just bought a KitKoin!"*

KitKoin again! It was weird how suddenly everyone was talking about it.

"It was really expensive, but if it keeps going up in value like it's been doing, I'll buy you whatever you wa— oh, sorry, Mrs. Moseley!" I heard aggravated mumbling in the background. "Gotta go, son! Molars to fill."

I hung up the phone, confused.

If Dad didn't get me the headset—and I knew Mom

hadn't—who did? But then I realized I didn't really care. I'd just have to make sure Mom didn't catch me playing it. Which I was going to start doing right now!

CHAPTER 18

What gall! When I entered the boy-ogre's lair, I saw him jumping up and down and waving his arms in a violent frenzy—wearing *my* VQ Ultra!

"GIVE ME THAT!"

I swiped his shin with my claws, leaving a trail of four bloody lines.

"Ouch!" he said, pulling his leg away. "What was that for?"

"Your skin is touching my technology," I said.

The ogre removed the headset and stared at me stupidly for many seconds.

"Wait—*you* were the one who ordered this?"

I swished my tail in annoyance. As if it were any of his business.

"You didn't use Dad's credit card again, did you?" he

said. "I told you, we could only get away with that once! And not for something that costs *thousands* of dollars."

"I did not use your father's plastic digits," I said. "I bought the headset with my own money."

I strategically ignored his many questions about how I had acquired this money, for he would surely want to share in my wealth. Meanwhile, I placed my head inside the device. It was awkwardly large, as it was made to fit an ogre's skull. (Strange that the Human brain is so big and yet so fundamentally weak.)

The helmet was nothing more than a monitor with headphones. The key was that it could be paired with the camera-enabled drone. Once I attached the Zom-Beam to the underside of this drone, I would be able to deliver my mind-controlling psylo-waves with perfect precision.

"Can I at least finish my game?" the boy-ogre said sadly.

Foolish Human. He thought this VQ was a toy,

when in fact it was the final piece of my ultimate weapon!

"Fine, you may 'play,'" I told him, removing the ill-fitting helmet from my head.

This, too, suited my purposes. I needed to see what else this VQ was capable of.

CHAPTER 19

I tried a bunch of different games on the VQ, but the ones that sounded the coolest were also too intense. The flight simulator made me want to barf, and *Zombie Dawn 8*—which I loved on my Z-station—was terrifying on the VQ. It was just *so real*.

Eventually, I found *Starista*, where you worked at a coffee shop and made lattes for people and stuff. It sounded lame, but it was fun to make milk-foam designs and come up with crazy-sounding drinks. And I made 271 star-dollars in tips, which was a lot more than the real dollars I'd made as a Gardeneer.

"So let me see if I have this straight, Human," Klawde said as he watched me play. "You dislike doing this thing called work, and yet when you can inhabit any reality you wish, you *choose* to work?"

"But it's not really work," I said. "It's fun! Look at how I steam the foam on this mocha chai latte."

It was really satisfying to hear the hiss of the steamer wand. And it looked so delicious!

"Riveting, truly."

Would all cats be as sarcastic as Klawde if they spoke English?

"Let me try my paw at one of these 'games,' ogre," he said. "Are there any battle simulators?"

"Tons," I said. "But they're really violent. And with the VQ, it's all a little too realistic."

Klawde didn't care. He put on *Bloody Combat Siege: Fall of Civilization III,* which was pretty much the goriest game ever created.

He was really good at it. His tail got all puffed as he played, and swished from side to side. An hour later, he had made it to the final level.

"That was amusing," he said, wiggling out of the gear.

"You could be a professional gamer, Klawde!" I said. "But you have to tell me—how did you get this system? It costs *so much money*. You got add-ons I didn't even know existed."

Klawde curled up on my bed and closed his eyes.

"You can't keep pretending not to hear me. You didn't sell any of Dad's sports memorabilia, did you? Or one of the cars?" I was suddenly panicked by the thought of all the things he could have sold. "If you don't tell me, I'll . . . I'll . . ."

"You will **what**?" Klawde said, daring me to threaten him.

"I'll . . . *pet* you," I said.

Klawde's eyes narrowed. "Well played, ogre," he said. He began to calmly lick a paw. "Have you ever heard of KitKoin?"

"Of course," I said. "Everyone's talking about it."

"I was, shall we say . . ." He stopped licking for a

moment. "An *early* investor in it."

"What are you talking about?" I said. "How?"

Klawde explained that he had opened an online KitKoin account using money I'd put in the bank after the garage sale, and that he'd bought twenty of the cyber coins when they were still worth one dollar each.

"But why would you do that?"

"Because by your standards—or any standards, really—I am a genius," he said. "Also, the name intrigued me."

"So how much are your KitKoins worth now?" I asked.

"Oh, roughly a thousand times what I paid for them." He went back to licking his paw.

I felt my heart skip a beat.

"Wait. Are you saying we're worth *twenty thousand dollars*?"

"No, ogre. I am saying that *I* am worth $19,980. You are worth $20."

"Hey, that's not fair!" I cried.

"Another most unfeline word. This tedious conversation is now over," Klawde declared, jumping off the bed and heading for the door.

"Will you at least buy me a skateboard?" I called after him. "And, like, a bunch of pizza?"

CHAPTER 20

I did in fact buy the boy-ogre a skateboard, which thrilled him, as well as a pair of "sneakers" to protect his soft, clawless feet. For some bizarre reason, they lit up with every step he took, the exact opposite of what sneaking is supposed to be.

These purchases were not made for his sake, but for my own. Occupied as he was with these new items, he left me alone to work on repurposing the VQ so that it would function seamlessly with the Zom-Beam.

The original Zom-Beam was intended to make Humans my servants via mind-controlling psylo-waves. But the Human brain, limited as it was in all areas of perception, simply malfunctioned when put under feline influence, as several unfortunate experiments with the father-ogre had proven. The simple command to fetch me a bowl of milk, for instance, resulted in him removing all his clothing (except, thankfully, for his small white undergarments) and squawking like a chicken.

The ogres having disappointed me as usual, I thus turned my attention to controlling a superior species: squirrels.

In my warlording days, I had often used these chittering rodents as mercenaries. I knew they reacted positively to psylo-waves, as this was how I had communicated with them in battle. Their reconnaissance skills were unsurpassed, and their supreme commander, Colonel Akornius Maximus, was quite possibly the fiercest—and most adorable—warrior I had ever known.

But I had run afoul of Akorn over a payment dispute. (How was *I* to know the difference between Gorgonian and Parnassian chestnuts?) In retaliation, the squirrel commander had had the nerve to try to assassinate me. Upon his fifth failed attempt, I forbid him and his troops from coming within a million light-years of Lyttyrboks, an act which he swore to one day avenge.

But enough about that fluff-tailed fool! I needed to attend to the task at paw. Namely, how to modify the VQ software so that it would allow me to mind-control an army of squirrels with maximum precision.

I called my minion and explained what I had learned from my experience playing the Human video game.

"Thanks to the VQ's motion sensors, every move of my body was mirrored in the battle simulator," I told him. Using a similar interface, I would be able to control a Zom-Beamed squirrel in the exact same manner. "But how will I control *more* than one squirrel?"

"Well, I can program a multi-squirrel mode," Flooffee said. "And instead of using the motion sensors, you can give verbal commands, like for the Zom-Beam."

He promised that the software upgrade would be ready within two moonrises. I could hardly wait. I had seen what space squirrels could do; it would soon be time to test the skills of those who lived on Earth.

CHAPTER 21

"Wow, that leaf-raking business is really going gangbusters for you, son!" Dad said as he got out of the Prius. "Look at that sweet new skateboard and those awesome new LED sneakers! Are you the coolest kid in Elba or what?"

"Uh, yeah, Dad," I said, kicking the board up into my hands. "The coolest."

"And is that a new smartwatch?" Dad asked once we got into the house. "Pretty soon I'm going to be asking to borrow money from *you*."

At a certain point, Dad was going to figure out something was wrong with this picture.

The doorbell rang, and Dad went to answer it. He came back carrying a stack of pizza boxes.

"Raj, did you order *three* pizzas?"

I had not. But I couldn't very well say that it must have been the cat.

"Um, yeah," I said. "One's for you."

Dad was about to ask me more questions, but the smell of pizza overwhelmed him. He took a box into the living room while I carried the other two down into the basement. I couldn't wait to play the VQ! Today I was going to try *Deep Space Explorer*.

Unfortunately, Klawde was using the system.

"Hey, can I have a turn?" I said, taking a bite of pizza.

He ignored me.

"Klawde," I said. "Can I use the headset?"

Still nothing.

I ditched my half-eaten piece and grabbed a new slice. Why get anywhere near the crust if you didn't have to?

"Seriously, *please*?" I said.

Klawde grunted.

I sat down next to him. "What's that game you're

playing, Klawde?" He didn't have the VQ plugged into the monitor, so I couldn't tell.

"Game?" he spat. "This is no game, ogre! This is . . . er, yes, I mean, of course it's a game. It is just so real it *seems* like it is not a game."

Klawde finally took off the VQ and stuck his head in the last box of pizza. He ate all the cheese off the top of the pie and then curled up on Dad's old La-Z-Boy to take a nap.

My turn!

I made it as far as the Kuiper belt in *Deep Space Explorer* before I decided to play something else. All that ducking of asteroids had made me feel a little nauseous. I cycled through games until I found one called *Pleasant Valley Junior High*. It was a middle school simulator, except that all the other students were icky lizard and squid creatures. It was awesome!

I'd just gotten put into detention for hitting my

science teacher in his head tentacles with a paper airplane when Cedar called.

"Are you coming or what, Raj?" she said. "We're here on Elbow Drive. The Three Gardeneers have a lawn to rake."

Shoot—I'd totally forgotten! But this eight-legged, pink-and-blue-spotted eighth-grader was passing me notes and the detention monitor totally wasn't seeing us. "A lawn to rake?" I repeated. "I'm, uh—*sniff sniff*—feeling pretty lousy. These allergies. My mom said I should take it easy and not do any outside stuff for a couple of days."

"Geez, Raj, I'm sorry you're feeling so bad," Cedar said. "But don't worry! We'll still give you your full share."

Suddenly I felt like a really horrible person.

"Oh, that's not fair," I said. "You guys should keep the money."

"No way. I'm not getting my telescope until you get your VQ," Cedar said. "We're all in this together."

"Just like the Three Musketeers!" I heard Steve yell.

I was almost about to turn off the VQ and go help them. I *was* feeling kind of sick, though. It probably had more to do with the six slices of pizza I'd eaten than allergies, but still. The thing was, I really wanted to go to the Pleasant Valley football game after school. I'd gotten picked to be on the cheerleading squad! I'd play a tiny bit more—just until my stomach settled—and then I'd go help them.

I put the helmet back on.

Whoa! The gym teacher who was running detention just molted his skin. This was **so cool**!!

CHAPTER 22

The boy-ogre had attended his virtual school so late into the night that he now risked missing his actual school. Honestly, who could comprehend what motivated these foolish beasts?

As a favor, I bit his toes in order to rouse him. Not that I minded; a warrior's jaws must remain strong.

The moment the ogres had vacated the fortress, I put on the VQ and selected *Really Hard Math*—the fake game I had created to mask the Zom-Beam program. (The title ensured the boy-ogre would never touch it.) Flooffee's new interface for the controls immediately popped up, and I was ready for my first trial run of the device.

From the comfort of my litter box command center, I launched the drone, which now had the Zom-Beam

attached to its underside. The drone exited the window of the bunker with a buzz and soared high into the sky. Ah, the joy! It was like I myself was flying, just as I had above the scorched battlefields of my youth.

I scoured the neighborhood, looking for my first pawn, and there she was: a sturdy she-squirrel, seated upon a branch, a nut in her nimble claws.

"ZOM-BEAM: STRIKE!" I commanded.

From beneath the drone came a whisker-thin laser. It struck the squirrel, bombarding her with psylo-waves. The controller automatically switched to single-squirrel mode, and I was able to direct the animal's every move as if her arms and legs were my own.

This was a most excellent first step. But I needed to test the squirrel in battle.

As if on cue, Wuffles, the neighbors' idiot dog, exited its fortress. The canine saw me—I mean, my *zombie*—and immediately raced toward us.

Oh, this will be delicious!

The canine leaped and clawed at the base of the tree, barking madly. I hurled the nut at the dog, striking the beast on its hideous snout. Wuffles looked momentarily confused, then started barking all the more.

"SURVEILLANCE MODE!" I commanded, toggling back to the drone's-eye view. I scanned the area again and selected two more specimens, which I struck simultaneously with blue-lasered Zom-Beams. Now all three rodents were locked into multi-squirrel mode.

"SQUIRRELS: SURROUND TARGET!" I ordered.

My trio now worked as a team. The two newer pawns snuck up on the dog from behind, while the original descended the tree. The mutt, suddenly realizing it was caught in a trap, tucked its tail between its legs and raced for the shelter of its fortress.

You are fast, Wuffles, but my squirrel zombies are faster!

The canine began to desperately scratch at the portal until the mother-ogre of his fortress opened it and the dog shot between her legs.

"SQUIRRELS: SCATTER!" I commanded.

The mother-ogre scanned her surroundings and then looked straight up into the camera of the hovering drone. Her eyes narrowed. It was almost as if she knew she was being watched.

Was it possible? Had I finally found a Human who was not a complete and utter simpleton?

It was highly doubtful.

CHAPTER 23

On the way to school, Cedar asked me if I was feeling okay. "Because—don't take this the wrong way, Raj—you look awful."

I wondered if there was a right way to take that.

"Yeah, totally terrible," Steve agreed. "No offense."

"It must be these stupid allergies," I said, faking a sniffle.

Actually, I only wished it were hay fever. Instead of going to help them do lawn work yesterday, I'd played *Pleasant Valley Junior High* until four in the morning and eaten all the pizza crusts I'd left in the box earlier. And I hadn't even touched my homework.

"Poor Raj," Steve said, slinging his huge arm over my shoulder and giving me a half-hug. "Cheer up! You know what the motto of the Three Gardeneers is?"

"*We rake with a smile,*" Cedar said. "Which was also your dumb idea."

"Oh, right—that's a good one!" Steve said. "But I meant the Three *Musketeers*. Their motto is *All for one and one for all*! Meaning I'll work twice as hard for you after school today, Raj."

That made me feel even worse.

"Maybe we should all take a day off," I said.

"No way," Cedar said. "We've only made $263 each so far, which means I'm still almost $700 away from getting my Astro 9000. And I know how bad you want that VQ."

I just nodded. My head felt sooo heavy.

"If we keep working hard, we'll be able to buy what we want. And earning our stuff will make it that much more satisfying to have," Cedar said. "Right, Raj?"

Well, that was what my mom thought. But my cat had made tens of thousands of dollars without even lifting a finger—or paw, I mean. And, anyway, I already *had* what I wanted. Did the fact that the VQ just appeared on my porch make *Pleasant Valley Junior High* any less fun to play? Not really.

"Uh, right," I said, and shrugged.

"Anyway, see you both after school at the Garcias'," Cedar said, heading down the hall to her homeroom. "I mean, assuming you're feeling okay, Raj."

"Yeah," I said, and pretended to wipe my nose.

I was trying to take a quick nap at my desk when I heard Miss Emmy Jo say something about KitKoin. I sat up. Her smiling face filled the entire smartboard screen.

"I mean, can y'all believe this newfangled money?" she said. "My husband, Fred, bought me one just because I love kitties. And wouldn't y'all know it, it's already worth twice as much! So I bought myself this cool new sweatshirt. See? It's a glitter kitty!"

All at once, everyone in homeroom started talking.

"My cousin owns like a hundred KitKoins," the kid next to me said. "And he says he totally knows the dude who started it—**Mr. X**."

"No way!" said the girl on the other side of me. "I heard Mr. X is this genius good-guy hacker. He's like a cyber superhero, and no one knows his secret identity."

Wow, KitKoin was a total phenomenon. And its value had doubled? Did that mean Klawde was even richer?

Maybe he could buy another VQ Ultra so we didn't have to share. Now *that* sounded satisfying, I thought, and I put my head back down on the desk.

CHAPTER 24

After an invigorating Strategy Nap, I conducted
more tests on my Earth squirrel pawns. First, I
investigated how many squirrels I could control
simultaneously; the answer appeared to be nine. Then
it was time to check their audio-visual capabilities.
Through a series of pop-up windows in the VQ headset,
I was able to see through the eyes of all of my zombies
at once. Finally, I tested my access to their ears.

"SOUND ON 8!" I ordered, selecting a squirrel
climbing up a tree.

Immediately, I heard what squirrel 8 was hearing—
the sound of the wind ruffling his fur, of his claws
scratching against the wood as he climbed, and of the
Humans walking below him.

". . . and then I was like, no, that is *totally* stupid, and he was like, no it's totally *not* stupid . . ."

"SOUND *OFF* 8!"

It was now confirmed. Like their cousins on other planets, these Earth squirrels would make perfect spies. As soldiers, however, they would be slightly less effective, as they were neither exceptionally strong nor correctly sized for using ogre weaponry.

Granted, a single squirrel could blind a Human, and groups of them could sow widespread panic, but it was doubtful that I would be able to conquer the planet—let alone rule it long-term—by such tactics alone.

Fortunately I had learned that in one area, Human backwardness could be turned to my advantage. As opposed to more advanced planets that used localized, renewable sources of power, such as stellar radiation and the vibration of subatomic particles, the ogres *burned things*. The electricity resulting from this barbaric burning of carbon-based matter was distributed across the planet using a jumbled system of wires strung up along the branchless trees known as "utility poles."

I knew that Earth squirrels naturally gnawed on these wires, occasionally causing local power failures. But by coordinating their efforts worldwide, I could interrupt the entire electrical grid—an act of sabotage that would swiftly paralyze this pitiful planet! Add in my soon-to-be complete control of the Humans' money supply, and it was as if Earth were already mine.

Purr.

But I would need far more than nine squirrels to put this plan into action. To conquer Earth, I would need a Zom-Beam that could broadcast psylo-waves across the entire surface of the planet.

OGRE ALERT! ON 6! OGRE ALERT!

I had posted a lookout squirrel to warn me of the return of my Human, whom I could now see walking home.

As I needed time to consult with Flooffee in the bunker, I would leave the VQ headset on the boy-ogre's sleeping platform—he never could resist escaping his reality.

But first, I would allow myself a little bit of fun.

CHAPTER 25

Talk about weird. I was almost home when a squirrel darted out in front of me and sat down in the middle of the sidewalk, blocking my way. I almost expected it to start talking—I mean, animals *did* keep doing that lately—but it just stared at me.

"You've got to get out of the way, little fella," I said. But then another squirrel appeared, right by my shoe.

Suddenly, both of them shot away, racing up a tree. I shook my head and started home again, but I stumbled and almost fell. *What the—?* Had those squirrels just managed to untie my shoelaces?

I looked up and saw they were still staring at me. It was creepy!

This was just one more reason that I wished this day was over. I'd fallen asleep in the back row of sixth-

grade math class and not woken up until eighth-grade algebra. I'd missed lunch in the meantime, and I couldn't even find the tiny bit of homework I *had* done.

Things didn't get any better when I got home.

It was a Wednesday, which was Mom's one afternoon off. That meant she wanted to spend time with me, so I got the usual barrage of how-was-your-day questions.

"I don't know," I said.

"How can you not *know*?"

Next came the what-do-you-want-to-do-this-afternoon questions. "Go to the science museum? Go for a hike? Play chess?"

I mumbled that I was supposed to go help Cedar and Steve, even though that was the last thing in the world I wanted to do. Well, except for everything my mom had suggested.

"Oh, Raj!" Mom called up the stairs after me. "Don't make any plans tomorrow. We're having dinner guests."

Dinner guests? My parents never had anyone over.

"Who did you invite?" I called back down.

"I invited Annie, the woman from across the street, and her adorable daughter. Lindy, is it? Annie has been so nice hiring you and your friends that I thought we should thank them with dinner," Mom said. "Besides, with her father and brother both away, poor Lindy must be lonely!"

All I could do was sigh.

I got changed and was ready to go meet Cedar and Steve, but I thought I'd better just check on *Jurassic Zoo*. It was this supercool game with brontosauruses and other sauropods where you had to feed and water them at least once a day and check the fences to make sure no raptors could get in.

Luckily, Klawde had left the VQ on my bed, so I didn't have to fight him for it. I adjusted the headset, which was already turned on.

But what was *this* game? It looked just like my neighborhood. There were trees and birds and cars and stuff, but I couldn't see anything weird or fun to do. I started clicking around, and I noticed that I seemed to be controlling a squirrel. But I couldn't figure out how to make it fly or shoot lasers out of its eyes or anything.

It was a seriously boring game. But it was *really* realistic.

And . . . was that our house?

I took off the headset and looked out the window. The squirrel—the one in the game—was on our sidewalk.

"KLAWDE!"

CHAPTER 26

"Heeyyyy, Supreme Master! I am so glad you called," Flooffee said. "I really want to ask you something."

"Minion, I did not call to hear *you* speak, I called to hear *me* speak."

I began with a full report on my Zom-Beam tests.

"It is all working even better than I had hoped," I informed him. "Colonel Akorn's mercenary squirrels may have worked for Gorgonian chestnuts, but these zombified Earth squirrels work for nothing at all! Akorn would eat his own tail if he saw what I was doing to them."

"He'd be sore at you for sure, O Masterful One." Flooffee smiled. "He always was cute when he got mad."

"So true. But, Flooffee, we must consider what our next step will be," I said. "Namely, how will we blanket the Earth in Zom-Beam rays?"

"We could launch thousands of drones," my minion offered.

"Well, of course we could, *if* these Humans had created any that worked better than wounded, geriatric birds. The one that I possess is so clumsy and of such short range it barely allows me to do anything at all!"

"How about a satellite?" Flooffee asked. "They must

have pawheld rocket launchers, right?"

I sighed. "Not even close. However, your suggestion does give me an idea."

Despite their technological shortcomings, Humans had managed to launch numerous satellites into orbit. These large, primitive devices streamed data down to Earth's surface using high-frequency waves. With modifications to their onboard software, these satellites could be made to broadcast psylo-waves——in other words, each one could become a giant orbiting Zom-Beam. The planet would be at my clawtips!

"Perhaps even in time for the greatest holiday in the universe," I declared.

Flooffee's ears pricked up. "Speaking of the Universal Day of the Most Supreme Leader, I wanted to ask you a little more about that—"

"Klawde!" the boy-ogre bellowed from above. Probably he wanted to show me something "way cool" in one of his tedious simulations.

Meanwhile, my lackey continued to babble on, but I had not heard a word.

When scheming global conquest, it is difficult to ignore two fools at once.

While the boy-ogre continued to call me, I cut off Flooffee. "Spare me your questions and start developing software that will work on Earth satellites. I will buy as many of them as is necessary to broadcast my Zom-Beams across this miserable planet."

"And you have enough of those dollar-thingies to buy all that?"

I scoffed. "Of course! I have as much money as I could ever need. For not only did I *create* KitKoin, I kept practically all of it for myself!"

I heard an unpleasant sucking of air behind me.

It was the boy-ogre. I feared he might have heard something he shouldn't have.

CHAPTER 27

I couldn't believe it.

I'd come down to the basement to ask Klawde if he'd been messing with the neighborhood squirrels, but I instead found out he'd created KitKoin.

It all made sense now! How could I not have realized? *Kit*Koin? An anonymous founder who was a *genius*? Who might be a *hostile entity*?

Of course it was my cat!

Klawde didn't own just twenty KitKoins—he owned the whole freaking company!

I must have gasped, because Klawde whirled around and glared at me. "How many times have I told you to knock, ogre?"

I had to sit down. "I can't believe it. *You* created KitKoin?"

"Yes," Klawde said.

"But . . . how . . ."

"It was kitten's play, really."

"Are you, like—" I paused before I could say the word. "A *millionaire*?"

"Don't be absurd. Of course not," Klawde said, swishing his tail. "I am what you earthlings call a *billionaire*."

"My cat . . . is . . . a **billionaire**?" I said. "THAT IS THE COOLEST THING IN THE UNIVERSE!"

"It is, isn't it?" Klawde said with a purr.

Then he scratched me. Hard.

"Ow! What was that for?"

"One, to punish the use of the phrase 'my cat.' Two, because I felt like it." He inspected his claws thoughtfully. "These do need sharpening."

I was really having trouble taking all this in. My cat—an evil alien entrepreneur! How had he done it?

What did it mean? And, most importantly, what could we do with a *billion dollars*?

The possibilities were insane! I could buy a whole new house and fill it up with everything I'd ever wanted! I could download every movie ever made! And put in a hot tub! We *definitely* needed a hot tub.

"We're so rich!" I yelled, bouncing up and down.

"No, *I* am rich," Klawde said. "*You* are still the same destitute beggar you were when you woke up this morning."

"Oh come on!" I said. "You used my computer, so you have to give me *some* money!"

"As if that piece of junk could create a cybercurrency!" he said. "While the idea was mine, the necessary computation and programming was performed by my minion on Lyttyrboks."

I rolled my eyes. "Fine. If you won't give me any, at least let me help you *spend* the money. What should we buy? A castle? An island? Oh wait—I know!" I said, standing up. "An ISLAND CASTLE. And a helicopter to get us there!"

Klawde flattened his ears back.

"Silence, ogre!" he said. "You are giving me a headache."

But I couldn't help myself. "Let's go to Europe! Or

Alaska—I've always wanted to go to Alaska. And we can't be selfish! Let's buy Cedar her telescope, and let's get Steve whatever it is he—"

Suddenly I remembered where I was supposed to be. With them. Raking.

I knew I should go. But I had to help Klawde spend the money, right? I mean, he was a spacecat. He didn't know what to buy.

I got out my phone and texted Cedar and Steve.

Sorry!!! I have to do homework. I'll be there for the next job, I promise!

CHAPTER 28

I had been hiding my extreme wealth from the boy-ogre, knowing he would bombard me with requests for extravagantly pointless Human trinkets, such as sparkling rocks called "diamonds" and large luxury motorboats. (As if any sensible creature would *choose* to travel on water.)

These Humans, they were so addicted to consumption. To shopping. To their possessions. Did they not realize that the most important things in life are those you cannot touch or possess, let alone buy?

Like power. And domination. And humiliating your enemies!

But there was another reason I had been loath to tell him, and it had to do with his most unappealing trait: fear.

I knew that once the initial thrill of riches passed, nervousness and panic would seize him. And so they did.

"Wait a minute, Klawde," he said. "Is this all . . . legal?"

"Of course it is." I straightened my whiskers. "Yes, *definitely* legal."

His contorted face told me he was not entirely convinced.

"All that stuff you ordered," he said, "it had *my* name on it. What if somehow people think I stole it? I mean, you may have started the cybercurrency, but *I* don't have any KitKoins. And what about your secret identity? You're Mr. X. What if they can trace you to our house?"

"Oh, don't be silly, Raj," I said in my most soothing voice. "I have thought of all such things. My existence is untraceable by Human means. Now, what was that you said about a helicopter? I believe there is a nice simulator on the VQ. Why don't you try it? To see if you want me to buy you a real one."

"Well, I *do* need to mop the floors at Starista," he said. "And I have an extra-credit assignment in *Pleasant Valley Junior High* that could get my grades back up."

"That's a good Human!" I said. "Run along, now. Run along . . ."

CHAPTER 29

"What? I can't hear you!" I hollered, taking off the VQ headset.

"Raj, our guests are here!" Mom called up the stairs.

Guests? Oh, right—Lindy and her mom were coming for dinner. And just when I was about to ask that mermaid from chess club to the school dance!

They were already sitting in the dining room, and Dad was bragging about how well my lawn care business was going.

"You should see all the things he's been buying!"

"*Shhhh*, Dad!" I said.

If he kept going on about all the money I seemed to have lately, Annie would think she was overpaying the Three Gardeneers. And worse, I might have to start working again. Because eventually *someone* would notice there was no way I could afford everything Klawde had bought me.

"But I am so proud of you, son!"

"It's wonderful!" Annie said, smiling her bright smile at me. "I figured you must be very busy with work and school and that's why you haven't cleaned the gutters yet. You didn't forget, did you?"

I was about to give her a lame excuse when Dad rescued me by telling a dentist story. Unfortunately, he kept telling dentist stories right up until we sat down at the dinner table.

"I tell you," he said, shaking his head, "you sure can learn a lot about a person by looking into their mouth."

"You can learn a lot about a person by looking at their computer, too!" Annie said. And then she winked at me.

I got embarrassed, remembering all of Klawde's weird searches. Then I thought, *I sure hope there isn't anything in there that has to do with KitKoin.*

"Did I hear that you work in computers?" my mom asked Annie.

"Well, yes," she said. She suddenly seemed a little shy.

"Where do you work?" Mom asked.

Annie took a long time to finish chewing her bite of spinach lasagna. "Well . . ."

"My mom works for the FBI," Lindy said proudly.

The *FBI*? I almost choked. I thought she worked at the Apple Store or something!

"I don't really like to say it because people can act sort of weird after I do."

"DON'T ARREST ME!" Dad said, putting his hands up and laughing dorkily.

Mom ignored him. "That's so fascinating," she said. "What's your area of expertise?"

"Cybercrimes, mostly."

I suddenly felt very hot. I noticed that Klawde had

come down from my room and was sitting on the stairs, his eyes fixed on Lindy's mom.

"Wow," Dad said. "What kind of cybercrimes?"

"I deal a lot with high-level fraud and financial theft," Annie said. "But what I'm

personally most interested in is cybercurrency."

Now I felt the extreme urge to leave. I caught

Klawde's eyes. He mouthed the words: *Be cool, ogre!*

"Speaking of cybercurrency, I got a KitKoin!"

Dad said. "I tell you, if I had bought a few more, I could quit being a dentist."

"Well, don't count on it *too* much," Annie said. "Every cybercurrency that's gone up in value has come crashing back down. Although, I will say, this new KitKoin is unique."

"Why do you say that?" I asked nervously.

"Well, the technology behind it is extraordinary, for one thing," she said. "Its encryption is like nothing we've ever seen. It's almost as if it uses *alien* technology. Whoever created KitKoin—the one they call Mr. X— must be some kind of genius."

Klawde descended the stairs to give her a leg twirl.

"Wow, he never does that to me!" Dad said. "He really likes you."

"But this genius," I said. "He's not breaking any laws, is he?"

"Well . . . ," Annie said, tilting her head to one side.

"The technology is so new, it's hard to say what's legal and what's not. At the Cyber Division, we have to keep track of alternate currencies, because sometimes they are used to fund criminal activities—or worse. If we find out that Mr. X is doing anything fiendish, well . . ." She paused to take a sip of water. "Let's just say I wouldn't want to be in *his* shoes when we catch him."

At this, Klawde fled down to the basement. I wished *I* could flee. Like, out of the country.

"But I should stop boring you guys with all this cyber stuff!" Annie said, taking a slice of garlic bread. "By the way, has anyone else noticed the neighborhood squirrels acting strange lately?"

CHAPTER 30

As usual, the ogres proved themselves to be the most misguided species in the universe, even at a dinner gathering. When it is time to eat, normal creatures put other concerns aside and do precisely that: They *eat*. Humans, on the other hand, *talk*, all but ignoring the food.

This conversation—as always—was mind-numbingly boring. Until, that is, a most fascinating topic came up.

Myself.

The neighboring mother-ogre revealed herself to be the officer of some kind of governmental agency that patrolled cyberspace. Perhaps this was why she'd recognized that my drone was surveilling her. More importantly, however, she recognized the immense genius of KitKoin and its creator.

It was now confirmed. This mother-ogre was the most intelligent Human alive.

Less welcome was the news that her agency was keeping a keen eye on KitKoin. I quickly went down to the bunker to take a Processing Nap. Unfortunately, the boy-ogre soon disturbed me.

"Did you hear what Lindy's mother does for a living, Klawde?" he asked in his most hysterical voice. "She investigates cybercrimes. For the FBI!"

"And what does that stand for?" I replied. "Furless Brainless Idiots?"

Humor, as usual, escaped him.

"The FBI are the people who put criminals in jail, Klawde!" he said. "And you put my name on all that stuff you bought with KitKoin. If the FBI figures out that the person spending all those KitKoins is also the genius behind it, they're going to think that **I** am the genius!"

"Oh no," I said. "No one will ever think that."

"And what are you doing with the squirrels?" he went on. "Annie was talking about them, too!"

"Squirrels? What squirrels?" I said. "You are beginning to sound a tad paranoid, Raj."

"I just don't want us to get into trouble." He looked down glumly. "I'm starting to think we should tell Annie everything."

"Do you mean *confess*?" I said. "A true warrior would never do such a thing!"

I could see, however, that he was seriously considering this action. So I decided to take a different tack.

"Look, Raj," I said as gently as I could. "I have done everything entirely according to your Earth laws. I have played by Human rules, and I am succeeding so massively for one simple reason. You are all stupid."

"So you *really* haven't done anything illegal?" he said.

"No, I have not."

Not yet, anyway.

Because—despite not having read the entire criminal code of all the various warlords of Earth—I did have to assume that using satellites to activate an army of zombie squirrels to take over the planet and establish myself as its eternal dictator must break a rule or two.

CHAPTER 31

I was working at Starista, trying to make a caramel mocha chai latte, but the machine wasn't working. I turned back to the person who had ordered it to apologize, but it wasn't a person at all. It was the gym teacher from *Pleasant Valley Junior High*. He had molted again, so he looked different, but I could tell it was him by the baseball caps on his two heads and the whistles around his necks.

All of a sudden, I heard sirens, and then more creatures were coming into Starista, but they weren't customers—they were sauropod FBI agents. I didn't know what I had done wrong, but I knew I was guilty anyway. They took me away in handcuffs, and my parents were there but they couldn't help me. And then I saw Klawde.

"Save me!" I said to him.

"I'm sorry, do I know you?" he asked.

Then I felt my toes getting bitten.

"Ow! Klawde!" I pulled my feet away from him. "Will you stop doing that?"

If it wasn't for Klawde playing alarm cat, though, I might've missed school altogether. I was *so* tired— not because I was up all night playing VR games, but because I was *dreaming* about playing VR games. And I got arrested in every single one.

Walking to school, I saw half a dozen squirrels hopping past me on the sidewalk. It looked like they were going to my house. What was Klawde up to with them?

Actually, I didn't want to know.

"You feeling any better?" Cedar asked at the corner where we met up.

"I think the answer is *no*," Steve said. "He looks even worse."

"Are you sure you should be going to school, Raj?" Cedar said. "This can't be allergies. You haven't helped us with the garden stuff in a week. Maybe you have the flu."

I wished I could have taken the day off, but the only thing my mom considered legitimate for staying home was hospitalization.

Just as we got to school, I felt the buzz of a text, and I fished my phone out of my jeans.

It was from Annie, Lindy's mom.

> There's something I'm VERY concerned about. Can you stop over after school?

Gulp.

CHAPTER 32

Finally, the most important holiday in the known universe had arrived! It commemorated the date of my birth, and was called the Universal Day of the Most Supreme Leader.

True, no festivities were planned this year—the Calico Queen had made them illegal, curse her—but I felt certain there would be spontaneous celebrations on Lyttyrboks among the legions of cats who remembered it fondly.

As a present to myself, I was going to purchase the satellites necessary to broadcast my Zom-Beams. I had found a network of them for sale, and the $12 billion price seemed quite reasonable.

But first, I would search the agent-ogre's computer. Once I accessed her wireless interface network, hacking into her device was pathetically easy.

I did this not because I shared the boy-ogre's panic, but because I thought she might have more nice things to say about me. And in her emails, I found that she had. I purred at being called *brilliant*, *deceptive*, *aggressive*, *corrupt*, and *sinister*. Who wouldn't?

I also read about how she planned to "put an end" to my scheme. While she might indeed be the most intelligent creature on this planet, she *was* an ogre, so I was hardly concerned.

Still, a warrior must be vigilant. This "Annie" needed to be kept under careful squirrel surveillance. I closed Raj's laptop and put on the VQ headset. The moment I did, however, I was met with something most unexpected.

A green flash.

CHAPTER 33

It was impossible to focus on school after getting Annie's text. What was she so concerned about? Did it have something to do with KitKoin? She couldn't possibly suspect who was really behind it, because he was a *cat*. But did she suspect me? Or my parents? Was she going to bring us in for questioning?

"Earth to Raj," said Sarah, the girl who sat next to me in math. "See that test in front of you? You should probably think about taking it."

What? I looked down at my desk. It was a pop quiz. I tried my best, but I could barely think.

What is $\frac{2}{3}$ to the sixth power? What is $13\frac{2}{9} - 9\frac{3}{16}$?

How was *I* supposed to know?

I was the last kid to turn in my sheet, and I took so long that Ms. Rice had already graded everyone else's.

She took a quick glance at my quiz and looked up at me. "Raj, you *know* that eighteen divided by two does not equal five. Are you feeling okay?"

That's what everyone was asking me these days. And even though I'd gotten the VQ and all this other stuff I wanted, the answer was always no.

The bell rang, which meant it was time to go to a super-boring assembly, and then an even more super-boring French class. (The teacher didn't even *know* French.) Still, for once I didn't want school to be over, because that meant I'd have to go talk to Annie.

CHAPTER 34

I had been sucked through more wormholes than I could count, but this time was different. Perhaps because of the utter surprise—or perhaps because I had been deposited *here,* on the cold, gray surface of what appeared to be a dead asteroid. I looked skyward and, to my shock, found myself gazing at the most beautiful sight in the universe: the magnificent planet of Lyttyrboks.

But wait—if Lyttyrboks was up *there,* that meant I was on one of the eighty-seven moons. And the only one this desolate was number thirty-six, notorious for its supersonic tornadoes and cat-eating yetis.

Why had I been brought here? WHO was responsible for this outrage? What kind of a **FOOL** would do such a—

"Happy Universal Day of the Most Supreme Leader, O Most Supreme Leader!"

Ah, yes.

"What have you done?" I roared at my minion. "I was in the midst of spying on my new nemesis! Send me home, you dolt!"

"Home?" Flooffee repeated. "But you can't go home! You're still Wyss-Kuzz the Butt-Sniffer."

"Not *that* home, fool. I mean Earth!"

"Whoa, you're calling *Earth* home now?" he asked. "Are you feeling okay, O Supremest? Earth's toxic atmosphere isn't finally getting to you, is it?"

"Earth will never be my home," I growled. "It is merely next on my list of planets to conquer. Now send me back so I can get on with it!"

"Look, your Excellency, Earth will be there for you to vanquish tomorrow—just like a billion other better planets in the universe," Flooffee said. "You're always working so hard on your evil schemes and all. You need to learn to relax a little. Particularly on your special day!"

My claws itched to slash him. "What part of 'send me back' do you not understand?"

"Come on," he said. "Isn't it kind of nice to be here visiting your favorite moon?"

"You idiot!" I said. "I told you moon *sixty-three* was my favorite!"

His eyes went wide. "Oh, right! I always do get those two confused. I thought it was kind of funny you'd pick the one with randomly bursting acid geysers."

I again demanded that he transport me back to Earth, and the fool again refused.

"There's so much to celebrate together!" he said. "Take a look at what I made for you!"

He stepped aside, and behind him I saw a—"What *is* that?"

"It's a statue of you!" He purred proudly. "It's made entirely out of butter!"

I peered more closely. The likeness was impressive.

I always *did* make a fine statue.

CHAPTER 35

Annie answered my knock right away. Her smile didn't look as bright as usual. "Hi, Raj," she said. "Thanks for coming. How are you?"

"Uh, fine," I said, even though I'd spent the last seven hours being worried.

"Good. Well, the reason I asked you here is a little strange. It's because—"

"Oh, *hey*, Raj!" Lindy said, coming out onto the porch. Usually I was kind of annoyed to see her, but right then I felt saved.

"Watch this!" She went over to Flabby Tabby and said, "Lie down, Chad!"

She beamed back at us. Neither her mom nor I had the heart to point out that the cat was already lying down. In fact, he was asleep.

"That's, uh, a great trick," I said.

"Want to see something else?" she asked.

"I need to talk to Raj," Annie said, interrupting Lindy. "About the, um . . . gutters."

The *gutters*? Phew—I'd been so convinced that it was about KitKoin!

"Oh yeah, sorry about that," I said. "I've been, uh, really busy. But I can get right on it."

When Annie and I went to get the ladder out of the garage, she said, "It's not really about the gutters, Raj. It's about what I found on your computer."

Oh no. My stomach tightened.

"After I had dinner at your house, I got to thinking about your search history," she said. "I have to admit, I thought you were fibbing about those searches not being yours. But then I got to thinking, why *would* a boy like you be looking up stuff like that?"

"Uh, I don't know."

"Not to alarm you, but I've seen evidence of surveillance activity around my house. And what's worse, someone hacked into my computer. I'm not sure how, unless they had hacked into *your* computer first."

My palms began to sweat. "How would *that* work?"

"Because you live across the street, your computer is close enough to get on my Wi-Fi network." She wasn't smiling anymore. "Does anyone *else* use your computer, Raj?"

I could hardly tell her that my cat did.

"Uh, no," I said. "At least, not as far as I know."

Annie looked like she was thinking it over. Then she smiled at me again. "Oh well," she said. "I don't want you to worry about any of this. If there are bad people behind this, we'll stop them."

I really had to get out of there. I turned to leave.

"But, Raj?" she said. "I still need you to clean the gutters."

CHAPTER 36

I wanted to tear him apart with my bare claws.

Flooffee had gotten me streamers. And balloons. And a clown robot to twist the balloons into animal shapes.

"This is not the Universal Day of the Most Supreme Leader!" I spat. "*That* holiday has the Running of the Hamsters! The Salute of a Billion Lasers! The Triumphal Road of Feathers! This—*this* is an **Earth birthday**!"

"But you were so fascinated by the party your Human had that I thought this was what you wanted."

"Fascinated by the *barbarity* of it, you imbecile!" I cried. "Now send me home—I mean, to Earth!"

Flooffee's face fell.

"Fine," he said. "I just have to do one last thing."

I swished my tail. "What is it?"

"Sing you a very special song."

I would do anything for this to be over with. Even listen to Flooffee-Fyr sing.

"All right," I said, gritting my fangs.

Flooffee purred. Then, he began to yowl:

Happy Universal Day

of the Most Supreme Leader to you!

Happy Universal Day

of the Most Supreme Leader to you!

Happy Universal Day

of the Most Supreme Leader,

dear Wyss-Kuzz!!

Happy Universal Day

of the Most Supreme Leader to you!

"That's not even the right tune," I hissed under my breath.

"What's that, O Glorious Leader?" he asked. "Did you say you liked it?"

"That is . . . *precisely* what I said."

That done, I turned to face my statue. It *was* handsome.

"Now, I will engage in licking my likeness until I have consumed all of this butter, and then you will return me to Earth so that I may complete its conquest."

"Oh, I don't think you want to lick that," Flooffee said.

"What do you mean?" I said. "Of course I do."

It was the *one* thing the dolt had done right.

I approached my own face—I could already taste the delectable butter—and licked at it. My tongue struck nothing. I tried again. And then I went to touch the statue. My paw went right through it.

"There's *no butter*?" I said.

"Well, it's not the easiest thing to get on this side of the universe," Flooffee said, scratching behind his ear. "And, you know, this *is* a simulation."

"What?" I said. "You mean this moon isn't real?"

"Of course not! This is your present—a *virtual* two-cat Universal Day of the Most Supreme Leader party!" Flooffee purred. "You're welcome!"

On the plus side, it meant that all I had to do was

take the VQ helmet off and this torture would be over.
But unfortunately, it also meant that I could not actually
tear my minion limb from limb.

CHAPTER 37

The stairs up to my bedroom seemed longer than ever. All I wanted to do was forget about the day and crawl into my bed, but my cat was hogging it.

"Hey, Klawde, move over and let me lie in my own bed for once," I said. "I've had a really hard day."

"Ogre, you have no idea."

"What was so hard for *you*?" I said. "You were in that same spot when I left this morning."

"You could not be more wrong. I was kidnapped. My idiot lackey opened a wormhole and transported me across the universe to a moon with acid geysers!" Klawde said. "And it *was not at all* just a virtual reality simulation."

"Wow—you went across the universe and you're back already?"

"Yes. I demanded that he send me back to Earth, and of course he always does precisely as I say." His eyes narrowed at me. "As all minions should."

"Wait a minute," I said. "You *demanded* to come back to Earth? Does that mean you like it here now?"

"Don't be ridiculous," Klawde snapped. "I came back to conquer it."

"What?" I said. "You want to conquer Earth?"

Klawde smoothed his whiskers with a paw. "Er, no," he said. "That is just an expression."

That was weird, but I let it go because there was something I wanted to ask Klawde about. "Annie thinks that her computer might have been hacked—from *my* computer. You wouldn't know anything about that, would you?"

"Of course not," he said. "Now I must go."

As he raced down to the basement, I got a funny feeling that my cat might not be telling me the whole truth.

CHAPTER 38

I was most annoyed. It was taking entire *days* longer than it should to vanquish Earth.

The fault lay with the ogres and their idiotic rules and regulations. Why did they have to make it so hard to purchase a dozen satellites?

I had already paid the $12 billion price in KitKoin, but I still could not take possession of them. Not until the end of what was called the "approval process."

It was infuriating. As if a warlord should need approval for anything!

Realizing I must not stay idle during this unwelcome delay, I cycled through all nine fundamental states of nap. It was in the final, most exalted state— the Nap of Knowledge—that I realized I had not tested the most important component of my plan. Could my

squirrel zombies effectively sabotage the electrical grid of the Humans?

I had to find a building on which to experiment. Although I needed a large target, I did not want to draw attention to my plans. Was there a structure that could suffer a power outage and no one would care? An institution of entirely pointless activity?

The answer came to me almost immediately.

CHAPTER 39

In homeroom, Miss Emmy Jo flickered onto the smartboard screen five minutes after the bell rang. She had a weird look in her eyes, and a shirt that was even more glittery than usual.

"Good mornin', Bookslugs," she said brightly. "Looks like I'm a smidge late!" Then she laughed—but it wasn't a nice kind of laugh. "Actually, I wasn't even gonna log in, but I figured I did owe y'all an explanation."

What was she talking about? An explanation for what?

"Remember how I said my Fred bought me a KittyKoin?" Miss Emmy Jo said. "Well, he actually bought me three, and they're worth so much now that this glitter on my sweatshirt is made from *real diamonds*." She downright cackled now. "I sure have enjoyed teaching y'all from a few thousand miles away. And I'm real sorry I never got to meet y'all in person, but that's the way the muffin crumbles." Then she threw up both her hands. "Aw, shucks, who'm I kidding? I'm not sorry at all! I'm getting richer by the hour, and **I quit**!"

Miss Emmy Jo was quitting because of KitKoin?

I wondered what she'd say if I told her that the creator of her cybercurrency was an *actual* cat.

Probably she'd like it even more.

"Since you're quitting," Brody said, raising his hand, "does that mean we still have to behave and everything?"

She leaned forward so her eyes filled up the screen. "Heck if I care! I've had enough of this here school thing. Let's have a—"

And then she was gone, right in the middle of a sentence. The screen had suddenly gone dark. In fact, all the lights had gone out, too. We just sat in our seats, stunned.

"Are we having a blackout because she quit?" someone asked.

"What are we supposed to do?"

Apparently, sit in the dark.

After about fifteen minutes, my history teacher, Ms. McQuade, came in. "What are you kids doing in here? Didn't you hear? The electricity is out in the whole school. There's some kind of problem with the power lines. You have the rest of the day off."

At that, everyone started cheering.

CHAPTER 40

The mission was accomplished with satisfying precision. My squirrel pawns chewed through the power lines of the boy-ogre's so-called school in minutes, then vanished into the trees like the ninja shadow raccoons of the planet Kleen 897.

After removing the VQ helmet, I contemplated a Victory Nap. But instead, I opened the boy-ogre's laptop and performed several vital searches.

> Earth satellite "approval process" time length

> why do ogres make everything so difficult?

> butter sculptor for hire

> crustless tomatoless pizzas near me

While searching for dinner, a messaging box popped up in the center of the screen.

I know what you're doing.

I felt the fur on the back of my spine rise up.

You won't get away with this.

Get away with what? Trying to find a pizza free of disgusting vegetables?

Your days are numbered, Mr. X.

Now *this* was interesting. I typed a response.

That is absurd. My days are infinite! Also, I despise that name.

What should I call you then?

I considered how much to reveal about myself. But for too long I had kept my true identity a secret in this dismal wasteland!

> You may call me . . . WYSS-KUZZ!

It now took several moments before the next line appeared.

> Do you mean WHISKERS?

> No, you FURLESS OGRE! I do NOT.

> Furless what?

I paused. I didn't want to give away too much. As the ancients say, *'Tis better to know your enemy than to know yourself.*

> Who IS this?

> It doesn't feel so good to be the one getting hacked, does it, WYSS-KUZZ???

Ah, so it was the agent-ogre from the fortress across the street! And she appeared to think she could challenge me. How preposterous! Still, it *was* nice to have an opponent—particularly one who had no hope of success. She typed another message.

> We are onto you and your sinister plans.

My paws flew like lightning over the keyboard.

> You have no idea how powerful I have become. I am one slight step away from TAKING OVER THE ENTIRE EARTH! And there is NOTHING you can do about it, Human!

I waited for a response, but none came. What was she doing? Well, I did have ways of finding out.

CHAPTER 41

Since school had ended about twenty minutes after it started, Cedar and Steve decided that we should go over to Annie's house early. Cedar wanted to finish bagging the last of the leaves, and we all were hoping for more cookies.

Baked goods aside, I wasn't excited to be there. I was still worried that Annie had somehow figured out about Klawde. But I was glad to be hanging out with my friends. I'd missed them. And as I scooped up leaves to put in the bag, it seemed like even my allergies were better.

"See?" Cedar said. "I told you it was the flu."

Yeah, the VQ flu, I thought. Maybe the cure was being outside. The *actual* outside.

When we were done, I rang Annie's doorbell.

It took a minute for her to answer, and when she did it was almost like she was surprised to see us. As she got out some money, she said, "Oh, shoot! I've been so busy with work today that I forgot to bake your cookie bonus."

"Oh, that's okay," I said, even though I was bummed. I'd been hoping for snickerdoodles.

Cedar and Steve hopped on their bikes to head home, and I turned to go across the street.

"Hey, Raj, can you hang back a moment?" Annie called.

I felt a knot in my stomach. What did she need to talk to me about *now*?

"I'm right in the middle of something on the computer so I only have a second, but I need to ask you a question," she said. "Does the term 'furless ogre' mean anything to you?"

My heart started beating faster.

"Uh, no," I said, trying hard not to sound like a liar. "Is that, like, the title of a kids' book or something?"

"No . . . ," Annie said. "Frankly, I don't know *what* it is. How about 'Wyss-Kuzz'? Does that mean anything to you?" Her face suddenly looked concerned. "Raj, are you feeling okay?"

No, I was not. "I'm fine," I croaked.

As I did, a leaf fell on my head. Glancing up, I saw a squirrel staring down at us, almost like it was following our conversation. It looked just like a furry gargoyle.

CHAPTER 42

Operating the Zom-Beam in single-squirrel mode, I was seeing through the eyes of a pawn perched upon a branch. From this vantage point, I observed the agent-ogre's attempt to interrogate my Human. I was pleased that he did not crack under the pressure; perhaps there was hope for him yet. Clearly, the agent-ogre had become obsessed with trying to stop me.

This, of course, was flattering, as nothing speaks to the brilliance of a powerful warlord like having a foe desperate to defeat them. Even a Human one.

I lost visual on the boy-ogre as he fled the agent-ogre and entered our fortress, but I heard the clomp of his footsteps as he came up the stairs. (Such noisy beasts, these ogres.) I removed the VQ helmet to find the Human staring at me with a stern look.

"Why hello, Raj," I said. "You're home early today. Was school less *electrifying* than usual?"

He looked confused for a moment. Then he shook his head and pointed at me. "Why was Lindy's mom— you know, the **FBI agent**—asking me about 'furless ogres'?" he demanded. "Have you been chatting with her online?"

I curled myself up on his sleeping platform. "Absolutely not. I swear on the life of my minion. I swear on *your* life."

"You're lying," he said. "And I know it, because you also told her your name was Wyss-Kuzz!"

I purred.

"Fine. It's true," I said. "I have been communicating with her. We are that special kind of friends known as 'enemies.'"

"She called you a *hostile entity*."

"I know—it *is* a nice thing to say about someone."

177

"I don't think you know what it means."

"I don't think *you* do."

The boy-Human groaned. "She's going to get you."

"She can't stop me."

"Stop you from *what*?"

There could be no reversing my scheme now, so why bother keeping it to myself? I told my ogre everything.

CHAPTER 43

When Klawde finished explaining, my legs practically gave out from underneath me.

My evil alien warlord cat was a billionaire tech entrepreneur who had bought a network of satellites so he could take over Earth with an army of zombie squirrels. And the one person who could stop him happened to live across the street and paid me to do her yard work, partly in cookies.

And people call movies unrealistic.

"But, Klawde!" I said. "Why would you want to conquer Earth?"

"I'm surprised by your reaction," he said. "I thought you would be happy that I am taking an interest in your planet."

"But what's—it's"—I stammered—"you have to—"

"Use your words, Human."

I took a deep breath.

"You can't conquer Earth, Klawde," I said. "You just
can't!"

"Except, in fact, I can," he said. "Why are you so
worried about it, anyway?"

"Why am I *worried*? Are you insane?"

"I won't do anything to *you*. You already serve me,"
he said. "You will be my number-one lackey."

"But not just anyone can go and buy twelve
satellites," I said. "They're, like, *in space*!"

"In fact, anyone *can* buy them," he said. "Provided
they have twelve billion dollars."

"Twelve billion dollars? You just spent TWELVE
BILLION DOLLARS? Wait—never mind," I said,
"because none of that matters. Lindy's mom is totally
onto you! You have to quit all this."

"As if I would surrender when I am on the very

cusp of conquest!" Klawde gave a single swish of his tail. "And besides, I am glad for the agent-ogre. Because what would be the fun of world domination if I did not have at least one opponent trying to stop me?"

Is it hot in here? I thought.

As I went outside, I passed my dad, just coming home.

"Hey, buddy," he said. "Where are you off to?"

"I need to get some air," I said.

For the next who knows how long, I wandered around my neighborhood in a daze.

Was I about to be arrested?

Was my *cat* about to be arrested?

Or was he going to succeed in taking over the entire world with an army of squirrels?

There were so many things to worry about, I didn't know which one to pick.

CHAPTER 44

Finally! It had taken another interminable Earth day, but the sale of the satellites had gone through, and I was in possession of the necessary access codes with which to control them. All that was left to do was upload the Zom-Beam software. I could hardly contain my glee!

I called Flooffee on the communicator. "Do you have the upgrade, minion?"

"You betcha, O Glorious One," Flooffee said. "I was stumped for a while on how to program these primitive Human satellites, but then I went to the ancient history museum and found some old feline ones of almost the *exact* same construction! I was able to use the same software, even though it was a couple hundred thousand years old."

"Fine job!"

I know—a good leader should never praise his underlings. But this was an extraordinary situation.

"I'm really anxious to see how this works," Flooffee said once the upload was complete. "I have to say, this might be my favorite evil scheme ever. I mean, squirrels! How cute is that?"

A purr vibrated through my entire being as I placed the VQ helmet upon my head. I engaged GLOBAL MODE, which would allow me to send all of Earth's squirrels on the same mission at once.

"3-D MAP!" I ordered.

At once, a spinning virtual Earth appeared, crisscrossed with lines representing the planet's power grid. All I had to do was give my zombie squirrels the command, and Earth's electrical supply would be cut, bringing the planet down to its hideous, hairless knees!

Purr!

"ZOM-BEAM: ENGAGE!" I commanded.

"SQUIRRELS: WORLDWIDE STRIKE!"

The effect would be instant!

Instant, I said!

Instant?

"So are you in control of Earth yet, O Lordly Master?"

"Shut up, fool!" I said. "Something is wrong!"

ERROR MESSAGE 692976

Curse the eighty-seven moons! What was the meaning of *this*?

"It looks like someone has taken all the satellites off-line," Flooffee said.

I threw down the headset in a rage.

Who could have done this? Ffangg didn't even *know* about this plan—nor did any of my other enemies. Well, except for—

No! It could not be! Not . . . a *Human*.

Was it even possible? With all the excitement surrounding Earth's conquest, I had neglected my surveillance of the agent-ogre. I glanced out the window toward her fortress, and there she was. Not inside of it, but standing on what the Humans call "the front lawn."

My front lawn.

There were other ogres approaching the fortress as well. Or should I say, invading my territory. All of them wore jackets bearing the acronym of Furless Brainless Idiots upon their backs.

This was an annoying development.

CHAPTER 45

"Can you babies shut up down there?" Scorpion yelled from his bedroom window. "I'm trying to finish level eighty-three of *Psycho Warrior 7*."

Steve, who was about to hurl a bunch of wet leaves at me, stopped. Cedar, who was sneaking up behind him with her own handful of slimy leaves, did the same. Obviously, we weren't supposed to be having a leaf war—we were supposed to be cleaning the gutters.

Scorpion kept glaring down at us. "Besides," he said, "don't you losers know that the *help* is supposed to be quiet?"

Cedar, Steve, and I looked at each other. Then we took our slimy leaves and hurled them up at Scorpion's window. We didn't hit him, but the look of fear on his face was awesome.

Being one of the Three Gardeneers, it turned out,

was pretty great, and work could actually be fun. You know, once you started goofing off.

All in all, I felt better than I had in days. The VQ had totally been messing with my mind. I didn't really have to pull a shift at Starista every day and Klawde wasn't really going to take over the world—he'd probably just gotten into the catnip again. And it wasn't like the

FBI was going to come arrest me.

We got ice cream on the way home. As we turned down my street, Steve pointed his dripping cone in the direction of my house.

"Hey, Raj," he said. "What are all those vans doing in your driveway? And why do they all have the word *FIBBIE* written across them?"

Uh-oh.

CHAPTER 46

The invading ogres appeared to be positioning
themselves for a paramilitary raid. While this was mildly
inconvenient, it would also be educational. After all,
I needed to study Human attack and siege techniques.

As the agent-ogres approached the front portal,
I wondered how they would enter. Would they kick in
the door with their massively powerful Human legs?
Disintegrate it with lasers?

DING-DONG!

They were ringing the doorbell? The fools! This was
not how you raided a fortress.

But the tactical error of the invaders would give
us more time to prepare our counter-strike. I considered
revealing my identity to the parent-ogres so we could join
forces in battle. But then I considered something else.

Why save them when I could simply save myself?

I quickly stowed the VQ headset in my litter box command center alongside the communicator, covering them both with sand.

Next, I ascended the stairs, only to find that the mother-ogre had willingly opened the portal to our enemies. Was she surrendering without a fight? I would have expected this of the father-ogre, but not her.

To protect myself, I assumed the disguise of an Earth cat.

"Me-ow," I said. "Me-ow. Me-ow?"

But I had no idea what to do next. Then I thought, *What would Flabby do?*

Of course! I should eat some disgusting kibble. Fearing my fangs would dull if I chewed the rocky pellets, I swallowed them whole. As I did, I chanced a glance up. No one was looking at me.

Could the Furless Brainless Idiots actually be

buying my ruse? Even when it was so obvious that **I** was the criminal mastermind of the fortress?

The neighbor-Human interrogated the parent-ogres. She had many questions

about Wyss-Kuzz, but my Humans simply shook their heads in confusion.

I realized I had underestimated the neighbor-ogre. Perhaps she was not worthy of the exalted title "nemesis," but she was a more able foe than I had given her credit for.

Audaciously, I approached and bestowed upon her the Leg Twirl, simultaneously complimenting and mocking her. Imagine her shock if she knew that the sinister genius she so desperately sought was right under her fleshy ogre nose!

Purr.

I wondered what plans she had for my Humans. Surely she would imprison them, and likely string them up by their flat fingerclaws. Or perhaps she would put them to forced labor. I doubted that they would ever again see the light of day.

Ah, well. Better them than me.

Thankfully, the boy-ogre was not at home. I hoped that at least he would evade punishment. After all, *someone* needed to keep the refrigerator stocked with dairy products.

The other Furless Brainless Idiots had by now swarmed the fortress, and they were removing various pieces of Human technology, such as the large flat device that the bald ogre sat ceaselessly in front of when he was home.

I only hoped they would take that hideous couch as well.

CHAPTER 47

I froze. What should I do? Turn myself in? How was I even supposed to do that—just stick my hands up? But what exactly would I be turning myself in *for*?

I watched as a pair of FBI agents came out of the house carrying our TV. They were followed by another agent—who was coming straight for **me**.

"Uh, we should probably go, Raj," Cedar said.

"Yeah, I think I hear my mom calling me," Steve said.

"Wait! Guys! Don't go!" I whispered to their backs.

When I turned around again, I found myself staring straight at the letters "F-B-I." They were stitched across the jacket of the agent, who was as big as a linebacker. I looked up, but instead of seeing his eyes I saw myself, reflected back in his mirrored sunglasses. It was terrifying.

The agent held up a badge. "I'm Agent Jacobson," he said. "Are you Raj Banerjee?"

All I could do was nod.

Then he pulled off his sunglasses and gave me a smile. "Pleasure to meet you!" He stuck out his huge hand.

It took me a minute, but I realized he wanted me to shake it. And it felt like he broke half of my finger bones when I did.

"If you'll just follow me, I think some explanations are in order," he said.

I gulped and followed him up the porch and into my house, where I found my parents talking to Annie.

And she was apologizing.

Annie turned to me. "I'm so sorry about all this, Raj. But once I realized that Mr. X—or Wyss-Kuzz, as he prefers to be known—really did hack into your computer to get to mine, we had to follow standard operating procedure. Which, I'm afraid, meant raiding your house."

While she went on explaining, I noticed that Klawde was sitting right next to her. He had a smug look on his face. Wasn't he at *all* worried about this?

"Now are there any questions you'd like to ask me, Raj?" Annie said.

"Well, um," I said, scratching my head. "Do you have any idea who this Wyss-Kuzz really is?"

"Me," Klawde said, "ow."

"I'm afraid we don't," Annie said, reaching down to pet him. "But whoever he is, he has almost unlimited computing and programming power. We could be dealing with a truly malevolent force."

Klawde began to purr and rub against Annie's leg.

"Wow, an evil genius using our computers?" Dad said. "That is so cool! I've never been so close to an evil genius before."

"But what was he trying to *do*?" my mom asked.

"Wyss-Kuzz—sorry, that name is ridiculous—secretly bought a network of satellites and uploaded dozens of encrypted programs to their onboard computers. These programs were so sophisticated we don't understand them yet. But we do know that they were designed to alter the waves that the satellites were transmitting."

"Fascinating!" Mom said. "And how did you connect the scheme to this Wyss-Kuzz character?"

"The satellites cost a billion dollars apiece, and the purchase was made entirely in KitKoin," Annie said. "The only person with access to that much of the cybercurrency was whoever created it."

The agent who had brought me inside interrupted us. "Mr. and Mrs. Banerjee, may I have your handheld devices?"

"You mean our iPads?" Dad said.

"I mean *all* of your devices, sir," he said.

Annie explained that nearly anything electronic we owned could have been hacked into, and that Wyss-Kuzz might have left clues to his identity on them.

My dad looked horrified. "Even my phone?" he said. "You can't mean my phone! And wait—not the TV?"

"It's already gone, sir."

"But why?" Dad said. "It's just a poor, innocent television!"

"It's also a networked computing device."

"Me-ow," Klawde said. "Me-ow, me-ow!" Then he rubbed up against Dad's leg.

Dad looked down at him in dismay. "And on top of everything, there's something wrong with Klawde."

"What do you mean?" Annie asked. "He looks like a normal, happy house cat to me."

"That's what I'm talking about," Dad said.

CHAPTER 48

As the ogres continued to speak, it became apparent that the agent-ogre and the rest of the Furless Brainless Idiots would not imprison any of my Humans. This was, I suppose, a positive development.

On the other hand, it was disappointing in the extreme to be deprived of my satellites. But as the great Si-Uh-Meez himself once said, *A planet too easily conquered is not worth conquering at all.*

I still did possess a vast fortune. And as long as I was the wealthiest being on the planet, I would also be the most powerful.

So, in truth, I had *already* conquered Earth.

Purr.

Then the agent-ogre mentioned something that concerned me.

"Because of what has happened," she said, "I expect KitKoin to experience a correction."

A correction? What did this mean?

"Well, I hope it doesn't correct *too* much," the father-ogre said. "Because I'm counting on that KitKoin to buy me an autographed Mariano Rivera jersey!"

No longer able to maintain my friendly feline disguise, I scratched the father-ogre. He was worried about his *one* KitKoin? What about my *millions* of KitKoins!

"Aww, Klawde, you're feeling better!" the father-ogre said, rubbing his wound.

I hurried down to my bunker command center. It was dangerous with the enemy still lurking about the fortress, but I dug up the communicator to check the LootCounter app.

I was relieved to see that KitKoin had reached an all-time high. Safe in the knowledge that I was growing richer by the second, I settled into a Contemplative Nap.

I napped many times that afternoon and into the evening, all of it gloriously uninterrupted by the boy-ogre. Sadly, such a blissful state could not last.

"Klawde? Klawde, are you down here?" he called.

As I yawned and stretched, I glanced again at the ticker app on the communicator. And I saw something I had never seen before.

1 KitKoin = 4.13 cents . . . 1 KitKoin = 4.08 cents . . . 1 KitKoin = 4.04 cents . . . 1 KitKoin = 3.97 cents . . .

Cents? What were cents?

"Ogre!" I called. "Are 'cents' what comes after billions in your primitive system of counting?"

"Um. No," the boy-ogre said. "Cents are worth *less* than a dollar."

I let out a yowl to pierce the upper strata of the atmosphere.

"But how could this have happened?"

"You should look at a news feed," the boy-Human said. "Every story is about how the mysterious founder of KitKoin tried to purchase a bunch of satellites for some totally evil purpose and it sent the value crashing. And they even use your name—Wyss-Kuzz. You're famous!"

My tail slashed in rage. As if I cared about something so insignificant as Human fame! I had lost my money—my *power*. Curse that agent-ogre and what she had done to me! Right now, she was surely baking celebratory snickerdoodles, gloating over this "correction." I would show her that Wyss-Kuzz the Magnificent was not beaten yet!

CHAPTER 49

I don't think I'd ever felt so relieved as when the whole FBI thing was over. Annie kept the raid of our house out of the news. She said it was "classified information," which I thought was awesome. I'd never had anything top secret happen to me before.

Of course, Annie couldn't stop people in the neighborhood from talking. Grumpy Mr. Wallace told everyone that we were being arrested for overcharging at our yard sale. And then there was school. I was just about to walk inside when I heard someone call me.

"Yo, Rat!" Scorpion said.

"Uh, yeah?"

"I heard the FBI raided your house," he said. "When did it become illegal to be a *loser*?"

He looked to Newt for a laugh, but instead she said,

"I actually think it's pretty cool."

And this time Newt wasn't pulling my leg. And other kids thought it was cool, too. It was like when everyone at school found out that I knew the author of the Americaman comics. Brodie saved me a seat at the cafeteria, and William bought me lunch—*and* remembered to make it vegetarian. Meanwhile, all the other kids wouldn't stop with the questions.

"What was it like getting raided by the FBI?"

"Did they have weapons?"

"Were there sirens?"

"No fair—I want to get raided!"

"Did you get handcuffed?"

"Were you scared?"

"Are you going to jail?"

It was kind of fun to be middle-school famous again, but I knew it wouldn't last. Anyway, all I really cared about was that no one in my family was going to jail. And though it was a bit of a bummer not having a cat who was rich anymore, I sure wasn't taking the KitKoin crash as hard as Miss Emmy Jo was.

She'd been back in homeroom that morning, and she was not happy about it.

"Dang that KittyKoin! I had to put my diamond-encrusted glitter-kitten sweatshirt up on eBay," she'd said. "If any of y'all want it, it's a bargain at seven thousand dollars."

I felt kind of bad for her. At least I was getting to keep my light-up sneakers. And my skateboard!

CHAPTER 50

I awoke from my sunrise nap, refreshed and re-enraged. Across the street, the agent-ogre lay snug in her fortress, certain that she had vanquished me.

But today I would send her a message—a warning that she could never rest peacefully. For as long as the squirrels of this zone were under my command, Wyss-Kuzz was far from defeated!

Soon I would put my zombified pawns to work. First, they would chew through her electrical wires. Then they would infiltrate her vehicle and disable its engine. Finally, they would turn their teeth to the fortress itself, nibbling holes in its roof until it was rendered uninhabitable.

Donning the VQ helmet, I sent the Zom-Beam drone aloft and entered multi-squirrel mode, selecting every tree-dwelling rodent within range. I quickly programmed their tasks and uttered the command, "SQUIRRELS: ATTACK!"

Within moments, a legion of squirrel zombies had descended upon the she-ogre's fortress. Oh how I loved controlling them! These fluff-tailed fools didn't even know they were being used! One by one they began to attack.

Then something went awry.

CONNECTION LOST CONNECTION LOST CONNEC

The error message kept repeating until every single one of my squirrels had been released from the Zom-Beam's control.

Suddenly a voice came through the headset—a voice I would know anywhere.

"Wyss-Kuzz the Vile! It has been many moonrises since we have spoken!"

Right before my eyes appeared a virtual 3-D image of he who hated me most.

Colonel Akornius Maximus!

"You!" I cried. "But how did you know?"

"We of the ShadowTail Confederacy have always kept watch over our Earthly brothers and sisters!" Colonel Akorn chittered. "Once we discovered this nefarious Zom-Beam and found out who had created it, oh, how I rejoiced in the opportunity to thwart you, you thin-tailed villain!"

"My tail is exactly the right size!" I said. "And even though you have just foiled my greatest evil scheme, I am unable to feel rage against you, because you are just SO adorable."

Colonel Akorn let out a squeak of fury and shook a tiny paw at me.

"You will pay for such insults! And you shall never again be left in peace. You dared use my squirrel brothers to spy on the Humans? Now they shall spy on YOU! What do you have to say to that, you oversized, long-whiskered feline?"

"What do I have to say?" I asked. "That you are even cuter when you are making threats."

He looked as if he were about to explode. And then, just as quickly as he had appeared, he was gone.

This was probably for the best. There was only so much cuteness I could take right now.

CHAPTER 51

With all of our devices gone, I was forced into a life of no screen time. Steve, in particular, felt bad for me. "It's almost like someone *died*," he said.

Honestly, though, I felt freed. In fact, I was pretty sure I never wanted to play another virtual-reality game ever.

"But I thought you wanted the VQ Ultra more than anything," Steve said.

I told him that I wanted something else more now. And after I explained what it was, he wanted it, too.

"The Astro 9000?" Cedar said when we got to her house. "You guys wanna chip in and buy the telescope I've been saving for—*together*?"

"Yeah," I told her. "I love space and stuff. And besides, between the three of us we've saved enough to buy it right now."

"And *you* agreed to this?" she said to Steve. "Did your brain catch Raj's flu or something?"

Steve shrugged. "I never could decide what I wanted to do with the money anyway."

Back at home, I found Mom walking around the house, rearranging the silverware drawer for the fifth time because her laptop was gone, and Dad sitting on the couch, staring at the wall where the TV used to be.

"Do you guys wanna go for a walk?" I asked.

My parents looked at each other like they didn't understand what I was saying. Then they turned back to me with a smile. "Sure!" they said.

I went up to my room to grab a sweatshirt. Klawde was on the windowsill, mumbling to himself and staring at a squirrel in a tree outside. The squirrel was staring straight back. And he looked kind of angry.

I guess Klawde really wasn't controlling them after all.

"*Akorn! Who would have thought . . . ,*" he went on mumbling. "*And a mother-ogre! I should have known. Mother-ogres are not to be trifled with.*"

"Sounds like you learned a lesson, Klawde," I said.

I had, too. Money didn't matter when you already had everything you needed. And I wasn't talking about computers, phones, or VR headsets. I was talking about family and friends. "And you, Klawde."

"Any more of your *sentimental values* and I'll cough up a hairball the size of a dwarf star!" Klawde said. "Be gone, idiot Human!"

"Fine," I said, and left to take a walk with Mom and Dad.

ABOUT THE AUTHORS

Although a worthless Human, **Johnny Marciano** has redeemed himself somewhat by chronicling the glorious adventures of Klawde, Evil Alien Warlord Cat. His lesser work concerns the pointless doings of other worthless Humans, in books such as *The Witches of Benevento*, *The No-Good Nine*, and *Madeline at the White House*. He currently resides on the planet New Jersey.

Emily Chenoweth is a despicable Human living in Portland, Oregon, where the foul liquid known as rain falls approximately 140 days a year. Under the top secret alias Emily Raymond, she has collaborated with James Patterson on numerous best-selling books. There are three other useless Humans in her family, and two extremely ignorant Earth cats.

Collect Them All!

"I cannot believe what you have just told me. My nemesis has failed in yet *another* evil scheme?" Ffangg said, purring into the communicator. "The fool cannot even conquer Earth? Oh my, how Wyss-Kuzz has fallen!"

"Yes, he is truly pathetic," Akorn agreed. "But even though I thwarted his plans, *still* he mocks me. That feline had better show me some respect at the next meeting of the Allied Warlords of Evil, or there will be much bloodied fur!"

"Even more than usual?" Ffangg said.

"If he calls me 'adorable' one more time—"

"Oh, I don't think you need to worry about what Wyss-Kuzz will or *won't* do at our next warlord gathering," Ffangg said. "A little birdie told me that Wyss-Kuzz is in for quite a disappointment."

Akorn narrowed his eyes. "*What* little birdie?"

"Blixbit, the vicious hummingbird of Mayhemique," Ffangg said. "He *is* in charge of the invites to the next meeting."

To Christina Hummel and
the Class of 2023—JM

For my dad, with love and gratitude—EC

For the late, great, animal-loving,
artist extraordinaire Laura Diedrick—RM

PENGUIN WORKSHOP
An Imprint of Penguin Random House LLC, New York

Text copyright © 2020 by John Bemelmans Marciano and Emily Chenoweth.
Illustrations copyright © 2020 by Robb Mommaerts. All rights reserved. Published by
Penguin Workshop, an imprint of Penguin Random House LLC, New York. PENGUIN and
PENGUIN WORKSHOP are trademarks of Penguin Books Ltd, and the W colophon is
a registered trademark of Penguin Random House LLC. Manufactured in China.

Visit us online at www.penguinrandomhouse.com.

Library of Congress Cataloging-in-Publication Data is available upon request.

ISBN 9781524787295   10 9 8 7 6 5 4 3 2 1